BEGINNINGS

Edited by Ann Walsh

Beginnings

Stories *of* Canada's Past

edited by
Ann Walsh

RONSDALE PRESS

BEGINNINGS

RONSDALE PRESS
3350 West 21st Avenue
Vancouver, B.C., Canada
V6S 1G7

Set in Minion: 12 pt on 16
Typesetting: Julie Cochrane
Printing: Hignell Printing, Winnipeg, Manitoba
Cover Art: Dwayne Davis, "In the Beginning," 19" x 14", mixed media:
   airbrush and chalk pastel
Cover Design: Julie Cochrane

Ronsdale Press wishes to thank the Canada Council for the Arts, the Government of Canada through the Book Publishing Industry Development Program (BPIDP), and the Province of British Columbia through the British Columbia Arts Council for their support of its publishing program.

NATIONAL LIBRARY OF CANADA CATALOGUING IN PUBLICATION DATA
Main entry under title:
Beginnings

ISBN 0-921870-87-6

1. Canada — Biography — Juvenile literature   I. Walsh, Ann, (date)
FC25.B44 2001   j971'.009'9   C2001-910607-6
F1005.B44 2001

Contents

Introduction

∽ *by Ann Walsh*

First there was the land, scoured by glaciers, swept by winds and battered by ocean waves. Huge, empty, cold, nameless. First there was the land. Then the people came and the stories began.

The stories in this collection are about young people from Canada's past. They are tales of courage and determination. They are stories of change, of something done for the first time — they are stories about beginnings.

Two First Nations stories are told here. In what is now Saskatchewan, a young Cree, Girl Who Hears Stones, hunts for berries by the shores of a yet-unnamed lake, listening to the faint sound of approaching horses. Much further to the West, on the shores of what will be Stuart Lake in what we will call British Columbia, a Carrier youth, Teluah, watches nervously as canoes bearing equally anxious strangers approach. For both Girl Who Hears Stones and Teluah, something new has begun; for both of them nothing will ever be the same again.

By the 1600s Europeans are settling the "new world". The men come first, then, when they decide to stay, they send for things which will make their lives and their work easier. Supplies, equipment and clothing come by ship from France. So do ships carrying cargoes of young girls, "filles du roi". These "daughters of the king" are to become wives of men who have already settled in New France, companions to comfort, to cook and sew, to work on the farm and, of course, to bear the children whose laughter will brighten the dark of winter.

Marguerite, an orphan, is one of these girls sent across the ocean to begin a new life as the wife of a strange man in a strange land. During the long ocean voyage, she takes strength from a half-heard voice whispering to her, "Courage, Marguerite".

There is the story of another Marguerite told here. Marguerite Sédilot is born in New France in 1643 — the same year a very young Louis XIV is crowned King of France and its colonies. The Sédilot farm nestles among ancient forests, rich with wildlife, and surrounded by waters teeming with fish. Although in 1660 the average age of brides in New France is fifteen, Marguerite Sédilot is only twelve when her name is entered into a contract of marriage. She is perhaps the youngest bride in Canada's recorded history, but she is also a very unwilling bride. She seeks courage to face her new life; she has little to turn to for comfort except a rare and wondrous "bear tree" on her father's farm.

Although there are many "brideships" leaving France in the 1600s, one ship carries a different cargo — horses, two stallions and twenty mares from the king's own stables. These are strong, sturdy animals, an ideal breed for the harsh climate and difficult working conditions of New France. The story of "The Little Iron Horse" tells of one of those mares and the young groom who accompanies her.

In the 1700s many new Canadians come, not from Europe, but from America. These refugees are the Loyalists who leave America because they want to continue living in a country that is a British colony, ruled by a British king. Loyalist families flee from the prejudice and violence of former friends and neighbours fighting for America's independence. They cross no ocean to come to Canada, but their journey is as dangerous and as frightening as a voyage through ocean storms. In the Mohawk Valley, one Loyalist family closes the door of their home for the last time and flees north, to safety. They leave behind not only their farm, their livestock and their dreams but also a part of their soul.

Over a century later, other families come from Europe. These homesteaders are promised land with bubbling streams, thick grasslands and even orchards in return for settling in Canada. They bring all their household goods with them; they also bring their hopes and dreams. What one family finds when they reach their homestead in Saskatchewan is a broken promise. Yet, as the oldest son, Dan, realizes as he stares across the wind-swept prairie, it is also the beginning of a new life, a life filled with possibilities.

A few years later another family, a miner's family, stand silent at a funeral in a village of the Crowsnest Pass. This area of Alberta is rich in deposits of coal which a growing Canada needs, not only to heat homes, but to feed the factory furnaces and stoke the railways' steam engines. Mining is a dangerous occupation. In the dark tunnels lurks a killer — methane gas. It is silent, invisible and explosive. Even if the methane does not ignite, it and other gases seep into mines and are poisonous to breathe. If a mine fills with these gases, miners must reach fresh air quickly. Many do not. Many die.

Two of the stories in this book are about the railroads whose tracks stitch our country together. Canada is so vast that, in the days before freeways and aeroplanes, railroads were a necessity. Although history tells us about the very last spike hammered in when the tracks from the east finally meet those from the west, we know nothing about who drives the *first* spike. Or do we? In "The First Spike" a young girl makes a connection with her family's past and wonders if she has uncovered the true story behind the railroad's beginning.

The early trains make little allowance for the comfort of their passengers. Travellers huddle on wooden seats, a wood stove provides the only heat, and any food for the journey must be brought with the passengers or purchased at stations along the route. In "A Gourmet Dines At The End of Track," a young cookee, or assistant cook on a railway work crew, helps prepare a special meal for the railway's General Manager, Cornelius Van Horne. This is perhaps the first gourmet meal offered in a railway car, although it scarcely resembles the meals that will later be served on fine linen tablecloths in the gracious dining cars of Canadian trains.

In the nineteenth century, children as young as five were considered legally able to understand the difference between right and wrong. This means that children, like adults, were held fully responsible for any illegal acts they committed and were punished severely. Although today we have a "young offenders" act, in 1845 young Antoine's gang of pickpockets are labelled "old offenders" by journalists. The oldest member of that gang is nineteen; the others are under twelve. Antoine Beauché, eight years old, begins a new life — in Kingston Penitentiary.

Other children, children whose families cannot support them, are sent to Canada from Britain during the nineteenth and twentieth centuries. These "home children" are placed in Canadian homes. Some are accepted as part of that new family; others become little more than unpaid servants who are offered little kindness and no love. In "To

Begin Again" one home child, Gwen, rebels against the treatment she receives when she begins her new life in Canada.

In 1919, another young woman defies her father and does what no woman of her family has ever done. She votes. It is difficult to believe that Canadian women could not vote before the First World War. Even when women won the franchise (the right to vote) they often discovered that voting was not considered an acceptable act for a respectable woman. "The Ballot" tells of how one woman challenges her father's belief that the women of *his* family shall never vote.

Another story from the twentieth century tells of a boy's dream of becoming a pilot. Before getting a pilot's licence, all trainees must solo, must fly without an instructor with them in the cockpit. In 1937, young Raymond Munro has completed his flying lessons and is ready to solo. Although the flight does not go well, it is the first step towards his future life as a pilot in the Royal Canadian Air Force and an award-winning journalist.

Some of the stories in this collection are about real people: Marguerite Sédilot, Antoine Beauché, Cornelius Van Horne, Raymond Munro. Other stories show fictitious characters living their lives much as real people of the same era did. From a Cree hunting camp, to the cramped quarters of a brideship, to an airfield near Toronto, these stories give us the flavour, the essence of what it was like to live in Canada's past.

Whenever we do something for the first time, we create a beginning, a new start. It has taken many centuries and many beginnings to make Canada the country it is today.

Gift of the Old Wives

A Story of Old Wives' Lake

ᴖ *by Beverley Brenna*

Girl Who Hears Stones carefully placed her birchbark box on the ground where the chokecherries wouldn't be spilled. Something wasn't right. She listened to the chatter of the other Cree women and children around her and the conversation of the four men sent to protect them in their search for berries. Under this comforting layer of voices was another sound, a faint thrumming that made the back of her neck prickle.

She picked up a small white stone from the sandy soil and rubbed its smooth surface. The noise grew louder. *Danger.* She looked around to see if Grandmother was near among the others gathering berries from the bushes by the lake. Grandmother was nowhere to be seen.

Fear tugged at her, pulled her closer to the stone for information.

"What?" she whispered to the white pebble. "What danger is coming?"

Blackfoot! she thought she heard the stone reply, along with the rising sound of hooves.

"Blackfoot!" she yelled. "Everyone take cover!"

The women and children reached for each other as their four guards jumped to attention, grabbing bows and spears.

When the men caught sight of the riders, however, they thankfully dropped their weapons.

"Mosquitoes are coming. Slap them, somebody!" one man called.

The band of boys on horseback, Mosquito raiders from their own tribe out to practise war moves, whooped and hollered, the ponies' quick hooves sending clouds of dust into the air.

Girl Who Hears Stones heaved a sigh of relief mixed with shame at her mistake. If the Blackfoot had come, she'd probably be dead already along with all her friends. But still, it was embarrassing to misunderstand when the stones spoke in her direction.

"Mosquito pests!" the women called. Three of the men sent to protect them in their picking laughed and pretended to strike at the boys' legs with switches.

"I know that horse!" called one of the men, suddenly. "Brave-eagle, get off my red pony. The mud you've rubbed

on her doesn't fool me. You and your jokes. Wait 'til I catch
you!"

The quick young rider turned the pony and charged
away from the angry man. Then he turned back, coming to
a sudden stop beside Girl Who Hears Stones.

Before she could move, Brave-eagle, in one fluid motion,
slid off the red pony, snatched up her container of berries,
and, grinning, jumped back on the horse, disappearing
with the other riders the way they had come. The owner of
the pony jumped on his brown mare and took off in hot
pursuit.

Irritated as she was by the loss of the berries, Girl Who
Hears Stones couldn't help but wish Brave-eagle luck in
riding fast, away from his pursuer. He was clearly the most
daring of the Mosquito pack.

She slipped the white rock into her moccasin, pushing it
under her heel so that each step hurt.

"Serves me right," she thought crossly. "I'll walk on this
stone all the way back to teach myself a lesson. I should listen more carefully when the stones speak!"

"Some warning, Girl," called Loose-leggings, one of the
three guards left. "I nearly sent an arrow over the bushes.
Might have hit your future husband, eh?"

"What future husband!" muttered Girl Who Hears
Stones, her face hot.

"Yes, thanks for nothing!" she heard one of the women
grumble. "The girl wants to stop my heart."

"Those kids, how fast they came upon us," said Grandmother, changing the subject. "What good warriors they'll make!" She picked up her berries. "Our baskets are full. Let's go."

Girl Who Hears Stones looked respectfully at Grandmother's feet, grateful for the change of subject. More people would have teased her, she knew, if Grandmother hadn't interrupted.

The other women nodded and everyone collected their things. Everyone except Girl Who Hears Stones. How could Brave-eagle have taken her box! She had worked hard to fill it, and Second Mother would be waiting. Early this morning they had gathered extra firewood, preparing to boil the berries, then crush and dry them in the sun. Later the fruit would be packed in rawhide bags, ready to take back to Qu'Appelle for their family during the moons when berries were scarce.

Time for collecting food was running out. Soon they would be moving the camp. Already the men had killed many bison near the lake and the women had prepared the meat for the long trek to Qu'Appelle where it would be shared among their people.

They knew it was dangerous for them here, hunting so far from home. But the Cree band had no other choice. Three moons ago a great fire had swept across the plains, its thick black wings chasing away the bison. The people followed the animals, moving west, until they reached this lake and again discovered the herd, contentedly grazing on unburned grasslands. It was either hunt here or die of starvation.

In addition to hunting, there was other work to do. After the bison had been slain, Girl Who Hears Stones had been responsible for turning the thin spirals of meat hung outside their tipi and for helping to keep the fire going with dry bison chips so that the meat dried thoroughly. She had also helped tie the strips of meat into small bales and then wrap them in rawhide so that they would stay dry during the journey home.

Now Girl Who Hears Stones looked at her crimsonstained fingers. What would she have to bring to Second Mother? Nothing. And besides the berries, she had also lost the box. She had made it herself, carefully sewing the sides with split spruce root and painstakingly decorating them with quillwork, just as Grandmother had shown her. She had even fastened a willow hoop inside the rim as a reinforcement so the edge wouldn't crack.

With heavy feet, Girl Who Hears Stones followed the others back to camp. As always when she had failed at an errand, she would have to endure Second Mother's sharp tongue. Not even Grandmother could pull silence into the tipi when Second Mother was angry.

It hadn't always been that way. When Girl Who Hears Stones had been small, her mother had been there to teach and gently correct. But she had died with the new baby, leaving her own sister to become Second Mother. And Second Mother had a temper unlike any other woman in the tribe.

It was Grandmother who took the time to teach her the things a young girl should know, and Grandmother to whom she went when something troubled her. But now Grandmother was far ahead on the trail.

"Why don't I have more sense?" Girl Who Hears Stones told herself. "Why didn't I listen more carefully? Now Brave-eagle's mother, not Second Mother, will be pounding my berries." The white stone inside her moccasin rubbed painfully under her heel.

Back at her tipi, she was surprised to see her birchbark box sitting on the ground outside the door, still filled to the brim. Brave-eagle must have ridden very skillfully, she marvelled, not to have spilled a berry. She looked around to thank him for returning her work and also for saving her from carrying home the heavy container, but he had vanished.

She pulled off her moccasin and emptied out the rock, ignoring a quiet voice that told her to wait, to listen again, and went to help Second Mother prepare the evening meal of bison stew.

After dinner, the elders met with the Chief to decide when the band should begin their move. Girl Who Hears Stones stood uneasily in the cool evening light, sniffing at the smoke from the sweetgrass smudges. What could be wrong? She tried to shrug off the anxious feeling as she saw her friend Pretty-bird walking towards her.

"I heard someone carried your berries home for you," said Pretty-bird. "Maybe you'll be married soon."

"Not likely," Girl Who Hears Stones answered.

"Someone gave my father a red pony today," Pretty-bird went on.

"Really? Who?" Surely it wasn't Brave-eagle, giving away the borrowed pony as another joke. Girl Who Hears Stones felt a twinge of jealousy. Why would he play such a joke on Pretty-bird? Did he like her?

"Running-fast. He said it was from his son." Pretty-bird smiled shyly.

"From Boy Who Walks Tall? Really? That means . . ."

"I'll have a husband soon."

The girls stood together for awhile, but as time went on, Girl Who Hears Stones began to feel even more uncomfortable. She walked around the camp, visiting now and then with other friends, until she caught sight of the lake. The water looked restless, foaming up against the shore although there was no wind. She walked down onto the sand and picked up the smoothest pebble she could find.

"Oh all right!" she said impatiently. "What do you tell me?"

She brought the stone to her ear and listened. For a few moments, all she heard was the tugging of the waves on the sand and the crying of a gull, flying overhead. Suddenly, the words came to her. *Blackfoot! Danger!*

Maybe the stone hadn't tricked her earlier after all, she thought, her heart pounding furiously. Maybe the Blackfoot really were coming.

Later, when Grandmother emerged from the Chief's tipi, Girl Who Hears Stones was waiting to walk with her back to their sleeping place. She said nothing at first about the stone's whispers but asked instead if she could braid Grandmother's long hair. As they sat close inside their tipi on the bison robe they shared with Second Mother, Father, and the half sisters — Small-deer and Little-flower — sleeping nearby, Girl Who Hears Stones combed her grandmother's long grey hair with the rough side of a dried bison tongue. After a while she spoke.

"I had another warning today," she said. "That makes two warnings about the Blackfoot."

Grandmother stiffened.

"Two warnings? Tell me."

Girl Who Hears Stones talked, at first feeling breathless, then relaxing as the story unwound. Grandmother always took her seriously. When she had finished, Grandmother turned towards her, looking worried.

"Blackfoot. Did you hear when they will be coming?"

"No. I should have listened more carefully, both times. It's all my fault."

"Try again tomorrow, early," said Grandmother, pulling some tobacco out of her pouch, "at the lake." Grandmother took out her clay pipe. Girl Who Hears Stones lay silent for a long time, feeling the smoke soft around her face. Then she slept.

The next morning when it was still dark, Girl Who Hears Stones and Grandmother went down to the lake together. They had to stop along the way because Grandmother needed to rest.

"Are you feeling sick?" Girl Who Hears Stones asked her as the old woman stumbled onto the salty shore.

"I feel my years," Grandmother answered, her voice competing with the sharp notes of water birds. "Last night I dreamed someone gave fishbones to the dogs. A very bad omen."

One at a time, Girl Who Hears Stones picked up and then replaced pebbles from the sand. None were any good.

"I can't hear anything from these," she told the old woman as the sun's light began to warm her face.

Grandmother stood still, facing the water, one of her hands closed into a fist. After a while, she turned and walked along the shore away from her grandchild.

Girl Who Hears Stones sniffed at the thick, salty smell of the water and watched a pelican circle above them, its great white wings rubbing at the sky, then folding, the bird dropping onto the surface of the lake, then rising again.

"We must go back, now." Grandmother took her arm. The urgency in the old woman's voice made Girl Who Hears Stones quicken her steps. Something really was wrong.

As they approached the camp, Cree scouts galloped past them and one man yelled for everyone to come and hear.

"Blackfoot," he cried, "Blackfoot scouts are nearby! They skirted the camp on fast horses, then galloped away!"

"Maybe they'll leave us alone," said Little-flower, running over to Girl Who Hears Stones. "Maybe the Blackfoot are too afraid to attack us."

"The Blackfoot are never afraid," said Girl Who Hears Stones. "I wish I had done more," she agonized. "I should have said something sooner to Grandmother." Suddenly, Brave-eagle was standing beside her. He touched her waist, then moved a step away.

"The warriors will attack at dawn. The Blackfoot always attack at dawn," he said.

Her hands and feet turned cold. The band had broken into small groups, everyone talking at once.

"Council members, meet in my tipi," commanded the Chief.

"It's all my fault!" said Girl Who Hears Stones. "I should have warned everyone!"

"You did your part." Grandmother touched her grand-child's arm. "You gave me time to think. Now it is my turn to act."

Before Girl Who Hears Stones could answer, Grand-mother had turned on her heel to follow the Chief.

"Mosquitoes, come with me," called Brave-eagle. "We will offer to fight with the other warriors."

Girl Who Hears Stones felt as though a spear had sliced through her stomach as she saw him stride off. Their band was small compared to the mighty Blackfoot. Anyone who fought would surely be killed. But, she thought again, anyone who didn't fight would also be killed. Her whole body cold, she looked over the people of her blood. All, she thought, all would be killed. She didn't need voices from stones to predict that.

After what seemed a long time, the Chief reappeared with the council members.

"Women and children, prepare to leave," he said to the gathering. "Take with you what you can. The men and almost-men will stay to fight the Blackfoot when they attack at dawn. Our council has decided."

The crowd muttered agreement.

"Make haste," he went on. "The day is passing. Soon the dark will be here to cover the women and children crossing the prairie."

Suddenly, Girl Who Hears Stones saw Grandmother step forward from behind the Chief.

"My Son," she began, "listen to what I have to say."

The people hushed at once, hearing her strong voice.

"The Blackfoot are many," she went on. "The men and almost-men staying here will be killed. The women and children who go on alone will have no one to protect them. They will have no one to hunt for them. The men will be dead and the women and children will die too. Our people will all die."

"Old Mother," answered the Chief, "there is no other way. If we all stay, we will be killed. If we all go, the Blackfoot will follow us and we will be killed. The men must stay and battle. The women and children must go. The council has decided."

"Listen to what I have to say," Grandmother said again. "I have another plan. A better way."

"What other way is there?" said the Chief. "If we all go, we will be killed. If some of us stay, you are right, those that stay will be killed. The Blackfoot are mighty. But those that leave will have a chance. The women and children will live."

"Travelling on their own, the women and children will die," said Grandmother. "Listen. I am old. I will stay. I and the other old wives, we will stay and keep the fires burning. The Blackfoot will come at dawn. They will see the fires burning. They will take their time. When they attack, our people will be far away. The Blackfoot will not follow. Our people will live."

There was silence in the camp.

"No," said the Chief, finally. "We cannot leave the Old Wives here to die. They gave birth to us. We cannot leave them behind. They deserve a better reward than death for their labour!"

From among the crowd, there was movement. One after another, old women came to stand beside Grandmother.

"Death is already close to us," said Grandmother. "We will stay."

"We will stay," echoed the other old wives.

"I will not run like a coward, letting my Grandmothers take my place in battle!" It was Brave-eagle, speaking like a man. Other men muttered their agreement.

"If we stay, we will die only once," said Grandmother. "But if you stay, we will die twice, once for ourselves, and once for you."

Everyone turned her words over in their minds.

"But who will teach our children and our children's children?" Girl Who Hears Stones' father eventually spoke. "Without your wisdom, how will our young people learn the Cree ways?"

"Our young people will remember what they have been taught," said Grandmother, looking at Girl Who Hears Stones. "Our young people are wise. They must now be given a chance to prove they are also brave. To be brave means walking toward life."

There was silence broken only by a mourning dove's haunting call. Then, one by one, the council members nodded. Finally, the Chief bowed his head in agreement.

"Prepare to leave," he said. "We will accept the gift the old wives are giving us. We will go at once."

Girl Who Hears Stones went over to her Grandmother. She looked down at the diamond patterns of the beads on Grandmother's moccasins. She remembered Grandmother, her head bent over those moccasins, sewing those beads.

"Hey, your grandchild thinks she's an old woman!" another old wife pointed and laughed. "Let's hear her bones creak!"

"Yes, let's see the riverbeds on her skin!" another called, grinning.

"I can't leave you here, Grandmother," Girl Who Hears Stones mumbled, her mouth dry. "I'll stay with you."

"We have earned this favour, Grandchild," Grandmother said calmly. "You have not."

The old woman reached out and dropped into her grand-child's hand a small, white stone, perfectly round.

"From the lake," said Grandmother. "It whispered to me. My old ears would not have heard it calling, but for you."

"You mean . . ." Girl Who Hears Stones couldn't find the words.

"You are not the only one who hears stones. Where do you think you got your skill for listening? Keep it safe, this gift. Safe for your daughter. Yours and Brave-eagle's." She chuckled. "Yes, I have eyes as well as ears!" Then she took two steps away from her grandchild. "Now go with your family."

Girl Who Hears Stones clutched the pebble, looked at Grandmother's beaded moccasins one last time, turned, and ran back to their tipi where she helped Father and Second Mother prepare for the journey.

As the last light from the sun flew like a white feather over their camp, Girl Who Hears Stones picked up the bur-den that was hers to carry and walked behind her half-sisters, following their parents and the others.

As she walked, Girl Who Hears Stones thought she heard a voice from the pebble Grandmother had given her and which she held inside her cheek where it would be safe for the long journey ahead. She couldn't make out the words, but she knew that it was Grandmother's voice speaking to her, telling her to be brave.

The taste of salt had long since gone from the pebble when Girl Who Hears Stones stopped for a moment to look at the stars. Each star was the soul of someone who had died. Grandmother had told her that. Soon, Grandmother's soul would take its place in the heavens, and look down on Old Wives' Lake, named in honour of the women left behind.

The rising moon shone on the figures moving eastward, blown like seeds across the prairie. It shone on the Blackfoot tribe, sleeping now, dreaming of war at dawn. It shone on the old women by the shores of the lake, wrapped in their blankets, tending the fires, waiting.

First Encounter

◦— by Margaret Thompson

This is a tale for two voices. Just as with music, there is no sense in listening to one voice alone, for that would be only part of the story, one side of the story if you will. And just as with music, sometimes the voices sing the same note, and sometimes they echo each other; sometimes they flow along different but harmonious lines, and sometimes they clash in the wildest discord.

But the tellers of this tale begin on a single note, in unison.

Both are sitting on the shore of a large lake. On our maps, the lake would be called Stuart Lake, and it lies at the heart of what is now British Columbia. That day was July 26, 1806, however, and if the lake had a name at all it was Na'kal Bun, and it had never yet found its way onto any map.

Our storytellers are sitting a quarter of a mile apart. Both are watching the sparks crack and fly in their camp fires, musing dreamily while the bats wheel in the dying light, and the sombre trees crowd closer. The water heaves and glimmers far into the distance, placid now that the wind from the north-west has stopped driving the waves straight onto the beach where the fires flicker.

In that still moment between wakefulness and the steep plunge into sleep, when conversation falters and the loudest noise is the snapping of the flames, our two storytellers turn in upon themselves and, without a sound, begin their duet.

Listen.

This started out just like any other day. Jean-Baptiste elbowed me awake at first light and I struggled out of my bedroll, rubbing the sleep from my eyes. As usual after a night stretched out on the ground, I felt as if I had been kicked all over. The river we had been struggling up for days was surging past, just a few feet away. It looked swollen and heavy, angry somehow, and the sky leaned over it, dark as slate. Another day of paddling, wet through and miserable, loomed in front of us.

I wasn't the only one concerned about the weather. Mr. McDougall was in a huddle with Mr. Fraser by the cold ashes of our campfire. As I went with the other boatmen to stow my belongings in the second canoe, I heard what he was saying.

"We should get to the lake by noon, I reckon, Simon. If this wind is still coming from the north-west, it'll be tricky," says he. "The canoes could be swamped. I've seen it happen before."

And he should know, if anyone does, for isn't he the only one who's ever been this way before? We're only here because he scouted the area six months ago and came back saying he'd found the very place for a fort, right on the edge of a great lake, salmon for the asking and beavers everywhere.

Back of beyond, I call it. Aren't there enough furs the other side of the mountains? Did we have to come to this wilderness? I can't see us ever reaching the Pacific Ocean, for all Mr. Fraser says there has to be a way, but then, as Jean-Baptiste never tires of telling me, I'm paid to paddle, not to think.

But Mr. McDougall's not often wrong, I've noticed, so I was prepared to believe him. I remember thinking, perhaps today we'll be able to stop and settle for a while, build a nice little cabin like we had last winter at McLeod Lake, and take it easy for a bit. I could do with a rest from paddling in the company of lunatics! Mr. Fraser's come straight from Bedlam, if you ask me, for all he's so highly esteemed by the Company.

This started out just like any other day. Grey, like the wolf, so I knew there would be rain. Not a day for picking berries, but we had time to mend the fish traps with spruce roots, and the women could chatter like the chickadees hiding in the trees as they went about their work.

I thought, if I was lucky and the weather held, maybe I'd catch some trout for my mother to cook over the fire tonight, but the wind picked up and I'll not risk my neck for a fish or two, even if my sister mocks me. "Teluah, you're as lazy as a winter bear," she says, but you won't see her out on the lake in a squall, either. No, life is too good to throw away and, besides, our cousin had a game of Lahal going, and I couldn't miss the chance of winning back the fur blanket I lost yesterday.

There's always another day.

All morning it was nothing but "Put your back into it, David!" and "Watch your stroke!" What did he think I was doing? Easy for him to sit there in the stern and give orders, Mr. High-and-Mighty Boucher, Mr. Fraser's lap dog, just because he knows how to speak to Indians in their own language if we ever meet any. He should try paddling this load for a while then we'd hear a different tune. By that time, the current was strong against us and we were near exhaustion, but then Mr. McDougall sang out, "This is it, lads, here's where the river leaves the lake!"

I snatched a quick look. An island dead ahead, and the water stretched far beyond it, but I didn't much like the look of it.

Behind me Hamish was muttering, "That wind's too strong; if the bowman doesn't look out and keep us heading into the waves, we'll be swamped before we know it."

That scared me. I'm not such a good swimmer that I'd relish a ducking any day and certainly not in waves like those.

Mr. Fraser was calling from the other canoe, but the wind was snatching his voice away. Mr. McDougall tried to yell back, jabbing his finger at the little spit of land ahead as if that was where we should head, but neither of them could hear one word in ten. It would have been funny, with them both purple in the face and waving their arms about like windmills, if it hadn't been so important to know what we were doing.

Then, as if we didn't have enough to cope with trying to keep the canoe on an even keel in that water, the bowman, James, suddenly cried out.

"What's that on the shore?"

I wanted to beg the waves to stop hurling us up and down for one second, just to let me see and know the worst.

"Hey," cried James as if he'd just spied an old friend, "could that be a crowd of people?"

Something was up. There was Toeyen racing around as if he'd been too long in the sun and cooked his head, shouting, "They're back! They're back! I told you they would come!"

Surely not, I thought. It couldn't be the white man again. Toeyen always said the white man promised to return and gave him that red cloth to seal the promise, but who listens to

*a crazy man who ties such a thing around his waist and boasts
how much he knows of strangers who appear and disappear
like ghosts?*

*But Toeyen had everyone stirred up, as if he had poked a
stick into a wasp's nest. All the children were running straight
to the lake, pointing and shouting. Some of them crowded
round the madman, getting in his way as he tugged and
heaved at an old dugout lying on its side at the water line. And
Kwah was beckoning, calling all the men together, sending
them off for bows and spears. That was enough for me. When
the Chief calls, I answer.*

*Two war canoes coming, someone said, bigger than any we
have ever seen, full of warriors chanting their war song.*

There certainly was a welcoming committee. Mr. Fraser
wanted to make an impression and I suppose we did, slicing through the water with the wind at our backs, Jean-
Baptiste singing his heart out, the paddles digging in to the
beat and everyone with any breath left joining in the chorus.

Suddenly, a flash of red caught my eye. Mr. McDougall
saw it, too, and at once he was pointing and shouting.

"It's the Indian fellow I met before," he cried. I remembered, then, he had told us about meeting one of the natives
while he was blazing the tree to mark the spot for the new
fort.

The man had to be crazy. Bobbing about out there like a
cork in those waves in a tiny dugout, waving that red rag as

if he'd shake off his arm. If we hadn't pulled him on board, he'd have capsized and drowned for sure. And that would certainly have impressed the others waiting on shore!

Betrayed! I heard the same word on every lip. Before we could stop him, Toeyen had leaped into the old dugout and gone to meet the strangers. Almost at once he disappeared into the trough of the waves, and then we saw nothing except in snatches as the water tossed him up before hurling him away again. I thought I saw him close to the two great canoes, but once again, whitecaps hid him from our view. Then Kwah pointed, and there was the dugout floating free back to the shore, empty, and Toeyen nowhere to be seen!

No time to lose! Kwah ordered us into line, weapons ready. The women and children ran to hide in the trees.

We were ready to give them a welcome they did not expect!

The Indian looked glad enough to be hauled over our gunwale, grinning and gibbering at us in his heathen tongue, pushing his red rag under our noses as if the smell of it would tell us all we needed to know. But straightway he was rearing up, waving and howling at his mates on the shore, till he was like to overturn us in his agitation. We paddled on through the din and the shore was getting nearer and nearer. We could see the people clearly at last and the sight was not reassuring. My entrails clenched and I had trouble getting enough air. Had he betrayed us? Were we heading straight into a trap? Why else would they have brought out their weapons? Oh Mary, Mother of God, had I come to this wild place to die like a stuck pig?

Well, perhaps we were hasty. Friends, said Toeyen, and there he was, sitting amongst them, smirking and mightily pleased with himself. Did the other men feel as foolish as I did, standing there in a line bristling like an angry porcupine with spears, with the eyes of our womenfolk boring into our backs and the children sniggering as if it were a game? But we could not be too careful. What did we know of their intentions?

To my relief, Mr. Fraser was not inclined to take the Indian at his word. Friends he said they were, but how friendly were those spears? Jean-Baptiste understood what the man was saying, but he couldn't tell if it was the truth. How did we know what their intentions were? Just as well, I think, that we beached the canoes at a little distance from the crowd.

It was just like Mr. Fraser to take the bull by the horns.

"We'll give them something to think about," said Mr. Fraser. "Out with the muskets, lads, and we'll fire a single volley over their heads. It'll do no harm and the noise will get their attention!"

So we dug out the guns and loaded them as quickly as we could, praying that the powder was still dry. I felt a whole lot safer with a gun in my hands, knowing that my companions were armed, too.

"Ready, lads?" asked Mr. Fraser, and we all shuffled into

line facing that hedge of spears and pointed our muskets into the air.

"Aim!" bawled Mr. Fraser. "FIRE!"

Aieeh! My head still reels from the voice of their weapons. When the pale strangers pointed them at the sky, their spears spat fire and cracked the clouds apart with thunder!

Maybe it was a bit *too* impressive! I guess they'd never seen guns before. Bang! went the guns and all the men flinched and clapped their hands over their ears, while the women-folk clutched at their children and cried out in alarm, huddling together at the edge of the trees.

Mr. McDougall looked worried, but Mr. Fraser was just plain exasperated.

"Make yourself useful," says he, giving me a shove towards the men who were clustered about their chief now, murmuring and gesturing at us. "Give them something, anything, get their minds off their fears! Look lively now, before this all goes bad!"

Well, all we had to hand was tobacco. Hamish and James and I edged over to the men, holding out the slabs of twist much as you'd hold out a bone to a dog you weren't quite sure of. We urged them to take the gift, but we were reluctant to go too close in case they took it amiss. It was a relief when one of them, a young man about my age, finally risked a look at me and closed his fingers round the tobacco I was practically forcing into his hand.

A gift of dried meat, but more bitter than spruce needles, fill-ing the mouth with vile dark water. Poison! I heard the dread-ful word whispered, but Kwah shamed the whisperers. "What reason would they have, these strangers, to be vengeful?" he asked. "Their ways are not our ways. Perhaps this food, so dreadful to our mouths, is as sweet to them as beaver tail is to us. Spit out the evil and cast it aside if you will, but let there be no insult."

How were we to know they'd think it was something to eat? I suppose it does look a *bit* like jerky. There was a lot more to worry about, though. The poor creatures were suffering, spitting the stuff on the ground and wiping their mouths, but it was easy to see from the dark looks some were throw-ing at us that they were certain we were trying to do them mischief. Mr. Fraser could stamp around all he liked curs-ing their ignorance, but he had to come up with a way out of this mess before the hotheads slit our throats!

What better way to smooth their feathers than to light up and show them how it *should* be used? Let them see that we suffered no harm? Then we could give them some of the clay pipes we carried and share a peaceful smoke like civi-lized folk.

"What fearful thing is this now?" my cousin whispered to me, and the women behind us murmured with a sound like the first stirring of the wind in the tops of the spruce trees. The strangers smiled, but their words stole out of their mouths

wrapped in smoke. I knew what my cousin was thinking, and others, too. Could it be? they were wondering. Could these be strangers from a country far beyond the edges of this world? Ghosts, with the smoke from their funeral fires hung about them still?

But it was plain to me they were no spirits. Too clumsy and awkward for one thing, and stinking like foxes, every one. No wonder when the poor fools travel without their womenfolk! And their chief — no lord of the other world would make so much noise, crying out and stamping his feet like a grouse in the spring. Besides, the smell of the smoke was sweet on the air. Have we not smelled much the same fragrance when the shaman burns his sweet grass? Their ceremony honours us, I told my cousin, and I cast about in my mind for a gift to honour the strangers and make them welcome. And I remembered the soopolallie berries my mother had gathered just yesterday to use in trade with our neighbours to the west.

What in the world was the matter with them? Some of them were smiling and nodding as we puffed away, but others gasped and moaned, hanging back and staring like owls as if we were something terrible. But then a woman edged her way through the ranks and shyly pushed a small basket made of bark at us. It was full of bright red berries, plump and juicy. We needed no encouragement to fall to with a will, I can tell you! Hamish and I scooped up a handful each and crammed them in our mouths.

Well, it was a case of the biter bit, and no mistake. Instead

of the luscious juice we were expecting, our mouths puck-
ered with a fearful bitter taste as if we'd taken a dose of
wormwood or gall. We longed to spit them out but one
look at Mr. Fraser's warning eye, and we gritted our teeth
and swallowed hard instead.

*One man's meat is another man's poison! Even the Chief
smiled as the strangers swallowed the soopolallie berries and
tried their best to look as if they were enjoying them. We
laughed behind our hands, and the taste of their sweet grass
no longer seemed so bad.*

Mr. Fraser was watching, chewing his lip as he listened
intently to Jean-Baptiste.

"Perhaps you're right," said he. "Maybe we'll get further
with the ladies. After all," he went on, sounding as if he were
trying hard to convince himself, "show me the woman who
doesn't like a present! If they're pleased, perhaps the men
will relax, too. How about some cakes of soap? I'll lay odds
they've nothing like that."

*When you have once been caught in a snare, you are careful
where you put your feet. The women were still wary when the
stranger who spoke our tongue beckoned them nearer. He held
out his hands, turning them this way and that so that the
women could inspect them, then he held up a slab of deer fat,
or so it seemed. "The strangers' gifts would be good," he said,*

"if you used them as they are meant to be used."

He dipped the fat in the lake and rubbed it between his palms until it foamed just as the soopolallie does when it is whipped in water.

"It cleans," he said, and then he shook his hands in the water again, and showed us, and yes, they were clean. Perhaps there is something to be gained from these strangers after all.

Now that worked a treat! Such a simple thing, but it broke the ice. What brought it back to me, I wonder? Perhaps it was the need to rescue Hamish from the woman who grabbed him and rubbed his arm with sharp sand till it was crimson just to show how she would clean herself. Or perhaps it was the sight of those children, naked as the day they were born, crowding about Jean-Baptiste as he demonstrated how to wash — just as if he did that regularly himself — and mesmerized by it. And their parents smiling at the children jostling round the stranger, even when one of them howled because she got soap in her eyes. What child isn't fascinated by bubbles? I took a piece of soap, lathered my hands and blew through my joined palms to make a big bubble, and the urchins round me cried out so that others turned to look just as the bubble wobbling on my hand broke free and drifted away on the breeze. That did it. Suddenly they were all trying it, all smiles, and even Mr. McDougall approved.

"That's a canny move, laddie," says he. "You seem to have

saved the day. Now perhaps we can draw breath. I'd like to try trading with them; one or two of them are wearing some bonny furs."

The stranger who knows our tongue spoke to Chief Kwah. He said his chief would give us many things if we brought him furs to trade. And when we asked how many furs he wanted, he told us as many as we could bring. I wondered what he could want with all those pelts when he had no use for the meat or teeth or claws. How will I earn the animal's forgiveness for taking its life if I do not need it? But he showed us what we could have: hard pots that will not burn on the fire; axes not made of stone, but shining and sharp, that bite deep into a tree; covers, not made of fur, but still soft and warm to the touch, and light; beads all the colours of the rainbow. But I wanted none of these. I had seen what I wanted and would face even spirits to get it.

When Mr. McDougall talked of trade, I did not expect to be the first to bargain. One of the young men, wearing feathers and porcupine quills woven in his long hair and precious little else, walked straight to me. He put his hand on his chest and said, "Teluah," so, assuming that was his name, I did likewise. "David." And I cocked my head on one side as much as to say, "And what can I do for you?"

Bold as brass, he pointed to the knife in my belt, and again to his chest.

I shook my head. Again his hand went to the knife, and this time he tried to pull it out of my belt.

"No, no my lad," said I. Not without something very good in return, I'm thinking, because that knife is the one thing I'd never want to be without. My thoughts must have been clear to him, for he looked downcast and slowly let go of the knife at my waist. Then he said something to me, made a gesture with his hand that I assumed meant I was to wait, and darted away. I didn't think I'd see him again, for we got the word that we were off to set up camp and settle in.

I could not hope that he would just give me the knife but I had little to offer in return. All I have is the drum I made from the skin of the deer my brother killed last year. I painted it with the sign of my clan, the bear, and I think it is very fine, but when I went to fetch it and held it in my hands, it looked a poor thing all of a sudden. Would it be enough, I wondered, for the stranger called David, who can send his spirit floating from his hands?

He was persistent, I'll give him that. Back he came with a small square drum and held it out to me, urging me to take it. I would have taken it, perhaps; it was a curious thing, much decorated with symbols that I took to be bears, and unlike any I had seen before. But Jean-Baptiste saw me hesitate, and stepped in smartly.

"Don't you part with that knife for such a paltry price," said he. "Could you afford to replace it? Don't forget we're here to set up a fur post. It's furs the Company wants, not drums! If it's a knife your friend's after, why, he'll have to go out trapping to earn it, and so I'll tell him!"

And he did, and all I could do was shrug apologetically when Teluah looked sadly at me. Business is business, I suppose, and Jean-Baptiste was right about replacing the knife — I'm penniless until we get paid at the end of the year — but you'd think they'd offer a bit more than beads to encourage these fellows to go out on the trapline.

They drive a hard bargain, these pale strangers. But it is a good knife. How easy it would be to skin a beaver or shape a spear or cut sinews with such a blade! And if the only way to get it is to take furs to the pale ones, then perhaps that is what I must do. But if we are to hunt in the winter, for the best furs, we shall need more traps and covering to protect us from the cold. Hide, too, for the women to make us moccasins and gloves. Where is that to come from? How is all this work to be done, when all our time is taken up already? I need to talk about this with my brothers, hear what the chief and the elders have to say.

The strangers have made their camp, just where the tall one marked the spruce tree all those moons ago. The shore looks different already: their great canoes drawn up on the beach, smoke from a fire curling above the trees, the beginnings of a lean-to being covered with spruce branches, boxes and bundles littering the ground. Already it is hard to remember it as it was only this morning: empty and silent, just the wind sighing in the branches and the waves rushing over and over at the shore.

The lake is the same. The trees are the same. The mountains and the islands have not moved. My mother and sister look as they have always looked. But much has happened today, so much that little pieces of it hide and will probably jump out to startle us when we least expect them.

In my bones I know that nothing will ever be quite the same again.

Amazing how these Indians can disappear. One minute they're milling around, chattering a mile a minute, the next, they've gone, vanished like smoke into the trees. Almost like a dream. Were they really here? Did I talk with one of them? Are *we* really here?

It's business as usual for Mr. Fraser. Nothing seems to ruffle him for long. I'm quite happy to sit here by the fire and keep the mosquitoes at bay, but he's already thinking out the next step, drawing plans for a fort with a stick on the shore, flailing his arm as if he would simply wave away the trees behind us, and arguing with Mr. McDougall.

Whether for good or ill, I'm thinking we have marked this place. If nothing comes of the fort and we leave no trace behind, perhaps we'll seem no more than a bad dream, or perhaps we'll fade into a legend that they talk about for generations. I wouldn't mind being a legend.

But if we stay, what will we be?

It's been a rum day and no mistake. Nothing out of the ordinary, I suppose, if you're an explorer like Mr. Fraser, but a rattling good shake up for plain fellows like me, and that Teluah, too, I reckon.

Since we arrived I haven't been able to shake the feeling that there are things going on that I can't see. It's like putting your ear to a clock and hearing the tick and the shudderings and whirrings inside, while there's nothing to see on the outside except for the big white face and the hands creeping round just as they always do.

Did something start today without anybody noticing?

Our storytellers fall silent, for it is dark and they are weary. Their last thoughts hang in the air and find their echo in the gentle rush of waves on the pebbles and their hissing retreat.

A beginning.

Nothing ever the same again.

And so it was.

Courage, Marguerite

∽ *by S.E. Lee*

The sailors' rough hands gripped my arms tighter. They needn't have held me with such force, I thought bitterly, I wasn't going anywhere. My throat constricted, holding back the sobs that threatened to erupt, as four sailors lifted the shrouded corpse from the deck. I knew if I allowed myself to cry I would soon be howling with madness like mother at the death of my baby sister.

Salt spray stung my eyes, a crude counterfeit of my unshed tears. The violently flapping sails drowned out the words of the captain as the sailors, their faces blank, lifted Jeanne's wasted body over the rails and let it drop. I heard a small splash that tore my heart, then the white package appeared, small and inconsequential, momentarily floating on the black waves before disappearing beneath the icy darkness.

No, they needn't have held so hard, for though I had an overwhelming feeling my own life had just been swallowed by the interminable ocean, I hadn't the courage to launch myself after my friend.

"Come, *mes filles,*" Mme. Goudron ordered, spreading her arms like the wings of an eagle before it dives. The other girls scurried from the scene like mice caught in the raptor's shadow. "Marguerite as well," she growled, motioning the sailors to bring me.

My feet felt as though encased in lead as I dragged them over the salt-stained deck accompanied by the sailors. We stopped to one side of the group. The sailors' muscular bulk isolated me from the other girls and young women, but less than did the knowledge I had been best friends with Jeanne. Though surrounded by other human beings, I'd never felt so alone, so afraid.

"*Mesdemoiselles,*" Mme. Goudron's imperious voice boomed, "Jeanne is in God's care now. It is time to think of the future. King Louis XIV and France are depending on you. Think of it. You, of all the young women in the care of L'Hôpital Général, were chosen for your strength of character to become the mothers of a new nation, a nation of people of strong mind, body and spirit. As *filles du roi,* you can hold your heads high. Now is the time, in this year of our Lord 1669, as we approach the end of this long and arduous journey, to think not of what has been, but of the glory that will be!"

I bit back a sour laugh knowing Mme. Goudron would have answered it with a sharp slap across my cheek. I'd felt the sting of her palm earlier that day when she had found me holding Jeanne's cold body and bargaining with the angels trying to take her soul. If she had just left me alone I might have saved my friend.

The sailor on my right turned and leered at me. His breath was foul, worse than the stench of the hold. I stiffened and moved away, making the sailor on my left grip my arm more firmly. Gritting my teeth, I stared ahead. There was no point in complaining; they'd just send me below deck to pray for my soul.

Had I really been a daughter of the king I would have ordered this *maudit* vessel back to France seconds after it had left the port of La Rochelle. I would have preferred to beg in the streets of Paris than suffer this pretence of strength and morality. Silently I cried out to Jeanne demanding to know why she had left me here all alone.

Jeanne, my source of courage and good cheer, killed by weeks of eating salt pork and dry biscuits, by vomiting and nausea, by sour water and poisonous air below decks. Damn her! It was her fault I was on this ship. How dare she abandon me like this!

"Come on, Marguerite," I could still see her lively blue eyes sparkling as she spoke. "Imagine! A new world, fifty livres, and our choice of husbands. We can create the life we want. What will become of us if we stay here? I can't spend my whole life in L'Hôpital Général and I won't let you either."

Staying forever in L'Hôpital seemed a good idea to me then and had I been able now I would have transported myself right back there. It was safe. It was the only safe place I knew in the world. I might even have become a nun, doing good deeds for unfortunates like myself and earning my place in heaven. Until the day Jacques and Guillaume, my two younger brothers, and I had been removed from the stinking streets where we'd begged to survive, life had been a blur of beatings and starvation. Our father had disappeared after beating our mother to death before my eyes. That was the day I began having visions and strange visitations. The sound of my father's drunken stumbling had followed him down the rotting stairwell leading from our rented room. I'd held my brothers' faces away from the scene and wondered what to do. Suddenly my mother's voice was whispering in my ear, telling me everything would be fine. After that I often heard her voice coming from unusual places, the strangest being when she'd spoken through one of the pewter tankards in the kitchen. The only person I'd ever told was Jeanne who'd laughed heartily and told me I'd be wise to keep that talent hidden.

L'Hôpital was not a palace, and I had missed my brothers terribly when they were sent to the boys' section, but there I had felt free for the first time in my life. I no longer had to worry about where our next meal was coming from. Gradually Jeanne had convinced me there was more to life than being safe. But now I thought she was wrong.

I looked across the prow of the ship. Still no sight of land. Maybe I would never walk on solid ground again. Was this a hope or a fear? At L'Hôpital I'd heard a rumour that Nouvelle France was full of Indians who hunted down the strangers in their land. There had even been a tale of a *fille* being captured by them. Was she still alive? Maybe she was a slave or had been given as a bride to some stranger with whom she couldn't communicate. Could that be any worse than what awaited us?

The relentless curve of the horizon remained as unchanged as it had for weeks. How could the earth contain such quantities of water? Maybe all the land had sunk into the sea and nobody on the ship knew. Maybe we would wander forever, searching and searching, but never sighting land, ending our miserable lives eating salty fish and drinking stale rainwater from moldy barrels.

A black shape broke the surface spewing water into the air with a loud "pheww". I watched the sun glinting across its immense back. The whales were the only good things I had found during the voyage. Their calm indifference to whatever happened above the water was strangely reassuring despite Jeanne's tales of whales eating ships and the people on them. Tell Jeanne I miss her, I whispered as it slid silently beneath the waves.

The voice of a sailor, or was it an angel, high above, caught my heart.

"Terre!"

The sailors ran from my side. I could move again but remained motionless as bodies shoved and pushed past me to peer over the railings. I didn't need to get any closer to see it.

"There!" One of the girls shouted, pointing to the west. I squinted against the steady glare of the morning sun. A thin, blue-grey smudge lay across the horizon, darker than the sky and lighter than the ocean.

The smudge grew rapidly as the next two days wore on. I spoke not a word, nor dropped a tear during that time, for who could I talk to about this emptiness inside me through which my fear swirled?

By the time the sun was sinking on the second day, a vast, dark continent surrounded our tiny vessel on three sides. With Mme. Goudron at my heels, urging me to get below deck for supper, I reluctantly followed the rest of *les filles* into the stinking hole below deck. Surrounded by the excited babble of the other girls, I fell into my hard cot, weary in spirit, afraid to hope the journey would be over.

Towards morning, after hours of tossing and turning, with my heart pounding harder than any wave that had beaten against the ship, I quietly crept past the sleeping forms of my companions and climbed the steep stairs to the deck. If Mme. Goudron caught me wandering around in the night without her permission I'd have to endure her vicious anger. And I didn't want to run into one of the sailors.

I peered cautiously over my shoulder as I tiptoed across the deck. To ward off the cold October wind sweeping down from the north, I pulled my shawl, a trousseau gift from one of the nuns at L'Hôpital, tightly around my shoulders.

The swish of the hull against the waves filled my ears as I stood, looking toward the future. Above me a strange, greenish, flickering light shimmered then disappeared. In the semi-darkness I heard whales blowing nearby. There seemed to be many. Were they surfacing to greet the morning?

The sun tipped over the horizon and a rosy glow lit the churning waves. My breath caught in my chest. We had travelled a great distance during the night and were moving swiftly in the middle of the river, surrounded by thick forest on either side. I looked in every direction but could see no sign of human habitation.

Suddenly a startlingly white object appeared in the distance. It floated on the surface of the water before disappearing beneath the dark waves. I stared across the water, searching.

There it was again — closer — but still too far off to see clearly. It was white and smooth looking very much like Jeanne's shrouded corpse before it was sucked beneath the waves.

Was she following me? Maybe she hadn't abandoned me after all.

I held my breath and clutched the rosary I'd taken from

my mother's body, whispering a quick prayer that it be true and I was not, as I feared, alone.

The familiar sound of a whale spouting made me look down. There, swimming effortlessly alongside the ship, was a small white whale. It lifted its strange bulbous head from the water and looked at me. It seemed to be smiling. Then it dove.

My heart dove with it. Is that you Jeanne? Come back. Don't leave me.

I leaned as far out from the vessel as I dared, searching the water for the white whale. The crests of the waves seemed to mock me — "here I am — no, over here . . ." I cupped my hand behind my ear, hoping to hear the whale's surfacing blow, but the roar of the wind in the sails, mingled with the groans and wheezes of the ship, drowned all other sounds. I searched the water frantically, praying the whale wasn't gone.

Cold despair washed over me and I ran forward, slipping on the salt-rimed deck. My hand grabbed the rail, such a frail barrier really, steadying me. Again my eyes swept the waters as fear and loneliness rose in my breast.

There. The whale's bulbous head reappeared below me. Its eyes seemed to sparkle as its smiling mouth opened. A sound emerged, high and bubbling, that reminded me of something. I could hear Jeanne laughing at my fears, telling me there was more to life than feeling safe. *Courage, Marguerite,* she'd said, her arm linked firmly through mine as we walked onto the ship.

My breath escaped with a sound like that of the surfacing whales as the white whale slid beneath the waves and disappeared. Though glad the apparition hadn't been seen by anyone else, I felt an ache of longing as soon as it was gone. Was it really Jeanne? Had I been witness to a miracle? Or was it some trick of the devil? I didn't care. Slowly, a quietness crept over me and I felt at peace.

The ship sped forward as if anxious to reach its destination. The river narrowed. I watched the water for the whale's return, but in vain. Once I saw a wisp of smoke through the trees and two small boats, canoes I believe they are called. I felt small, like an ant caught on a leaf floating in a stream, as the forest-covered land pressed in on me, and I wondered where my place would be in that immensity.

A short while later a voice shouted *"Québec!"* from the crow's nest, startling me from my reveries. I wondered if the sailor had seen the whale speaking to me.

Ahead a tall cliff stood guard over a clutch of dwellings.

From below deck the rumble of feet clattering up the stairs announced the arrival of the rest of *les filles.* The deck was soon filled with the excited chatter of girls crowding around. Mme. Goudron, emerging last from the ship's hold, had never noticed my absence.

"Regardez," said one of the young women, a widow, who'd never had a kind word for those of us from L'Hôpital. She looked haughtily down her nose at the settlement. "There are hardly any houses. And they are so rough and unpretty. What kind of life will we have here?"

I barely heard her. The sun on the changing trees made them glow red, orange, and yellow behind the small settlement. And there, on the dock, milled dozens of smiling faces. My face felt suddenly hot. Somewhere in that group of people might be the man I would marry. For that was the purpose of the journey, was it not? But how would I endure it? I had no idea what kind of man he would be. What if he beat me as *Papa* had beat *Maman*?

Jeanne's voice echoed in my head. *"Courage, mon amie..."* I could endure it. I wasn't alone. I scanned the faces on the dock. No man would ever beat my children, nor me. I would do my best to choose my husband with care. Jeanne would help me. I lifted my head and squared my shoulders.

I looked back toward France. The fear and timorousness that had gripped my past dissipated like fog off a river when the sun strikes it. In the distance a white shape bobbed up.

Ignoring Mme. Goudron's steely gaze, I waved to it. It dove and flipped its tail into the air as if waving back to me, then I turned and prepared to place my feet on the foundation of my new world.

As I stepped onto the ground, strangely solid after weeks at sea, a tern flew over my head. In its cry I heard Jeanne's voice calling me forward toward adventure, telling me it wasn't the end, it was the beginning.

The Little Iron Horse

ᴘ— by Anne Metikosh

Odd, that in three months aboard ship, amid the shouted commands of the crew, the slapping of waves against the hull, the crackling of the sails, the sound he remembered most clearly was the beating of his own heart. It was nerves, of course. Pierre knew that quite well. Père Lucien, the priest, would have called it conscience had Pierre gone to confession. But he had not. What would have been the point? He had no intention of confessing to anyone what he had done.

He had been amazed and excited to learn that King Louis, the Sun King, intended to send a small herd of horses to the colony in New France. He knew, of course, as everybody did, that the colony was vital to France. The King's taste for waging war and throwing lavish parties to celebrate his victories was paid for by taxes that had beggared the people and depleted the country's resources. New France was so rich in furs and fish that building up the colony could only benefit them all. Three years ago the King had sent soldiers to settle the fur trade wars against the Iroquois. When the peace treaty was signed, he granted many of the soldiers land in the new world to encourage them to settle there. Now, in the year 1670, he was sending farmers and tradesmen and *filles du roi.*

With all the building and clearing and ploughing to be done, the settlers would need horses.

Two stallions and twenty mares from the royal stables were to be shipped to the new world, along with several grooms to care for them and oversee their breeding once they arrived. Pierre had begged for the chance to go. In France he could never hope to rise higher than the post of stable assistant. There were too many other willing young men, with too many better connections. In New France, he would be one of only two such *palefreniers.* Even if he had not wished to go, his skill and his understanding of horses meant that he was one of the first to be chosen.

His favourite mare, Génie, was not. A six-year old warmblood, she was a great pet among the ladies of the court, admired for her sweet nature as much as her graceful stride. They did not want to let her go. Pierre could not bear to leave her behind. She had been his special charge since the day she was weaned from her mother. He had fed her, groomed her, trained her for others to ride. How many times over the years had his breath caught at the vision of sunlight gleaming on her elegant head? Had there ever been a day when his throat did not tighten at the sound of her gentle, welcoming whinny? She was his Génie, in fact as well as in name. He could not imagine a new world without her. But how could he possibly get her there?

"If you were truly a génie," he whispered, tickling her ear as he combed out her forelock, "I could spirit you into a bottle and carry you with me in my pocket." He stroked her face, running a gentle finger down the white strip that ran from the star on her forehead to edge of her nose. When she was born, the marking had looked more dramatic, like a puff of smoke rising to take the shape of the phantom for which she had been named. But as she matured, its outline blurred against the finely chiselled bones of her face and now drew attention not to itself but to the warm brown eyes that framed it. Pierre hugged Génie's neck and blinked back tears. She ducked her head, curving her neck to rub her face up and down Pierre's arm in mute sympathy.

After a minute, Pierre felt her nose stretching farther, aiming for the pocket of the jacket he was wearing. He laughed. "I know what you're after, you clown. You think I have carrots in there." Génie gave him a bland, innocent look. "Well, you're not going to get them for nothing. You'll have to ask nicely." Pierre imagined he could hear her sigh of resignation as she lifted her right foreleg, curling it up in a courtly bow before accepting the treats she obviously felt were her due.

"What an actor you are, princess." Pierre was still chuckling as he threw Génie's blanket back over her and bent to buckle the chest and belly straps. Then the laugh died in his throat and he straightened slowly, staring first at the blanket and then at the white marking on Génie's face. An actor, he thought. An actor wears a costume and makeup. He gave a triumphant little shout. Génie looked startled. Pierre gave her a reassuring pat, then put a finger to his lips and leaning very close he murmured, "I've got a plan!"

After weeks of preparation, the day of departure dawned grey and drizzly. Light fog hung in the air like ghost's breath, dampening the spirits of the courtiers who had planned to picnic on the lawn as they saw the horses off, and sending them scurrying instead for the fire. The grooms who came to help load the animals hurried head down from task to task, cursing the weather and drawing their hat brims low over their eyes. Pierre saw his chance to claim Génie, and he snatched it.

Génie was a mid-size bay. Apart from her face marking, there was little to distinguish her from many of the other mares in the stable and they were all blanketed against the chill in identical royal blue and gold rugs. The courtiers could only tell one from the other when the horses were presented in their brightly hued and highly individual tack. Each had its own saddle pad of brilliant blue, red or green, embroidered with multi-coloured birds and flowers and hung with gold tassels. The saddles were plain, but the bridles were tooled with fanciful designs, and ribbons to match the saddle pad were braided around the leather straps. The grooms, of course, could tell the horses apart at a glance, but the grooms were not paying any attention to Pierre that day. They were too busy and too anxious to be inside, out of the miserable weather. It was the work of an instant to substitute Génie for one of the approved colony mares. Pierre had practised this sleight-of-hand many times in the preceding weeks. It was rather like juggling, he thought, moving Génie to an empty stall, another mare to Génie's stall and then Génie out of the barn altogether. No one noticed what he was doing; no one shouted at him to stop or to put the horse back where she belonged. Best of all, even Jean-Luc, the *valet d'écurie,* said nothing as he checked off names against the list he held.

Did Pierre imagine it, or did Jean-Luc pause to look hard at Génie? The *valet* had been watching him closely the last few days, Pierre was sure of that. Had he noticed that Génie's white markings had been slowly darkening? Had he seen the bottle of dye that Pierre brought with him to the stable every day? Was it conscience, Pierre wondered, that made his stomach clench and wouldn't let him meet Jean-Luc's eye? They had been friends a long time, but if Jean-

Luc suspected Pierre of so grievous an offence as trying to rob the King, would he hold his tongue? Did he suspect anything at all, or was he merely being careful of his job? Pierre's hands were shaking when Jean-Luc finally told him to proceed and he led Génie away from the royal stables toward an uncertain future.

On board *Le Roi de la mer,* there were just three of them to look after the horses, the same three that would look after them in New France: Pierre, François and Jean-Luc, who, as *valet d'écurie* spent most of his time with the stallions. François, the other *palefrenier,* was a taciturn sort of fellow. He spoke rarely and then only to the horses. Pierre preferred it so. He did not want to draw anyone's attention. At first, he felt sure that as long as no one noticed his deception until after they had sailed, all would be well. Later, he told himself that surely the captain would not turn the ship around for the sake of a single horse. But day after day, throughout the long months of the voyage, his palms still sweated at the thought of what he had done.

Ten weeks later, Pierre was beginning to wonder if he would ever see land again. For what seemed like the thousandth time, he made his way along the deck behind the line of mares, scooping up muck and throwing it overboard. Stopping next to Génie, he gently patted her muzzle. There was plenty of extra hay for her now. They had lost two more mares during the night. That made eight dead now. Six had sickened over the course of the journey, worn down by the constant motion of the ship and the confined quarters. Then, last night, a storm had blown up quite suddenly, setting the ship rolling even more wildly than before. Two of the horses had panicked, setting back on their hocks and straining to snap the lead ropes that held their halters. They had snapped their necks instead. Their carcasses had been stripped of meat and heaved over the side.

It was both difficult and dangerous caring for so many horses for three months aboard ship. The stallions were not faring too badly. Kept separate as they were from the rest of the herd, and given that there were only two of them, they were easier to feed, water and shelter than the dwindling group of mares. It would have been foolhardy to allow them access to the mares while at sea. Breeding was a violent exercise — the rolling deck and slippery footing could only be disastrous. So the stallions were quartered on the foredeck. The mares were kept aft. Pierre had tried to rig canopies to shelter his charges from the salt spray and the wind, but the canvas bagged and sagged so much with every gust that the effort was futile. He mourned the six who had died. The others were getting weaker by the day. Their coats were thin, their eyes growing dull. Landfall was the only thing that could save them.

Pierre was becoming increasingly anxious about Génie. He spent long hours at her side, willing her to survive, crooning to her, "Come on, my princess, you're a brave, strong girl. We haven't come this far for nothing, little one. Wait till we get there! Think of the hay you will have to eat, and the open spaces to run in! Don't give up, my Génie!"

Pierre was growing thin as quickly as the mare. Guilt and worry consumed him. If he had left Génie behind, he thought, she would be safe now. If she died, it would be his fault. And how would he ever bear that burden?

That they were getting closer to their destination, Pierre was certain. The waves carried clumps of grass, and seagulls cawed raucously overhead. Through a fine veil of mist, Pierre glimpsed the shadow of an island that must be the fabled Ile des Démons. Even at that distance, he could hear the strange, ululating cries that echoed around it and he felt a chill run down his spine. Beside him, Génie began to fidget nervously, nostrils flaring in alarm. "Don't worry, my pet," Pierre murmured. "There's nothing to be afraid of. It's only a story. A Paris legend, do you see? They say that over a hundred years ago, the soldier pirate Roberval abandoned his niece and her lover on that island. The lover died; the poor girl was eventually rescued by some fishermen and taken back to France. But her spirit stayed behind and now they say the place is haunted." As he talked, Pierre gently stroked Génie's neck, quieting her fears. "I don't believe in ghosts, do you? No, of course not, we only believe in génies!"

The next day, the first mate announced that they were entering the Gulf of St. Lawrence. The gulf was so wide that

Pierre had the sense they were still on the high seas, but they had already passed the rocky coast of Newfoundland and slowly the northern shoreline of the St. Lawrence river became visible, some of it grassy, some forested. The horses became restive. Where they had stood listless for so long, bracing their legs hard against the pitching of the deck, now they shifted in their places, whickering gently to each other, their nostrils flaring as they breathed in the clear, fresh scent of the new world.

And at last they reached Québec. Pierre took a deep lungful of air and let it out with a gasp. He felt as though he had been holding his breath for the entire voyage. Now he could hardly contain his excitement. "We made it, Génie. We did it! Back in France they will be saying only that we made a mistake and took the wrong horse. Too bad. Here, no one will know the difference. Even Jean-Luc, if he notices you don't look the same as you did when we started, can hardly say anything now." Pierre smiled as he ran his fingers over Génie's face. He had run out of dye weeks ago and Génie's star and strip were showing more clearly every day. The actor's makeup was wearing off.

The waterfront at Québec was crowded with storehouses and docks where three-masted sailing ships disgorged loads of cargo, passengers and news. Small wooden boats plied the waters of the St. Lawrence River, the great highway of New France. *Le Roi de la mer* bumped gently against the quay and erupted in a flurry of activity as the sailors on board tossed lines to those on shore, who made them fast and secured the gangplank. The captain and Jean-Luc were first to disembark. They were met on the pier by an impressive looking gentleman dressed in the frilled white shirt and decorated red coat of an aristocrat. Pierre noticed him from the deck of the ship. "Look, Génie," he joked, "a human peacock!"

"That must be the Intendant, Jean Talon," came an excited whisper at Pierre's elbow. Pierre startled at the voice, so unaccustomed was he to hearing François speak. Perhaps the new world would lend François new voice, he thought. Aloud, he said, "The Intendant is the man in charge here, isn't he? He will be able to tell us where to stable the horses."

The stallions were the first to be led down the gangplank, and they skittered on the unfamiliar footing before finding solid ground on the pier. Pierre watched as Jean-Luc took off his hat in the traditional salute to the governor of the colony, but somehow effacing himself and his skill as a horseman and presenting only the horses. They were magnificent, one from each of the most renowned breeding provinces in France: Normandy and Brittany. The Breton horse was the smaller of the two, but noted for his soundness and vigour. The Norman horse was not totally unlike, but showed something of its Andalusian ancestry in its feathered legs and the abundance of mane and tail. It was a pity, Pierre thought, that the fashion at the French court was to cut the tails short. Maybe here in New France, they would be allowed to grow to their intended length. That would give some protection at least, against the hordes of flies that apparently plagued the inhabitants of the colony in the summertime.

And now it was time to offload the mares.

Several of the sailors moved to assist Pierre and François as they untethered their charges. On the dock, the crowd had grown to include the passengers from another ship, eager to see the horses. The spectators were mostly young ladies, Pierre noted, probably *filles du roi,* sent by the King as wives for the farmer settlers in the colony. One in particular caught his eye. She was small, with an abundance of curly brown hair and startlingly blue eyes. When she realized that Pierre was staring at her, she blushed modestly, then sent him a smile that made him wonder if perhaps he, too, might find a wife here in New France. The touch of a warm nose on his hand distracted him from his reverie. Génie was tired of being ignored. It was her turn to descend the gangplank.

The surrounding woods and meadows were just budding into June flower when Pierre, François and Jean-Luc settled their charges into their new quarters. The stables were not nearly as grand as the fine stone buildings they had left behind in France, but they were a vast improvement over the rolling deck of the ship. And if the rough wooden planks that shaped their stalls signalled a change in station from playthings of the rich to animals with a destiny to fulfill, the horses themselves did not appear to mind. These few were to be the foundation stock of the colony's herd. They would be used for breeding, not for clearing the fields or dragging heavy plows. During the summer months, they would be free to roam the woods and eat their fill of the rich meadow grasses.

June was late for breeding. Gestation lasted eleven months, which meant that the first foals would not be born until the end of May. Early April would be better. It would give the newborns a longer start before winter set in, but Pierre knew that they could not afford to wait another year to begin.

Not all the mares would catch, of course, and for those that did not, they would have to wait until spring to try again. Knowing her as well as he did, Pierre was sure the time was right for Génie. He was anxious to breed her to the Breton stallion, Caillou, sure that his strength and her fluid movement would produce something very special indeed.

Jean-Luc apparently agreed. Whether out of friendship or a breeder's reluctance to leave such a quality mare behind, he had never openly accused Pierre of stealing the horse, nor had he commented on the disappearing and reappearing markings on her face. For that Pierre was grateful. All the same, Jean-Luc had given him an uncomfortable few minutes when he stepped off the ship with

Génie. Staring hard first at the horse and then at Pierre, Jean-Luc had said ironically, "Funny, isn't it, how alike some horses look?"

By December, the full weight of winter had descended on New France. Snow whipped the landscape, first greying it, then turning it blinding white. The river stilled and froze in the intense cold. As far as possible, people huddled indoors by their fires. Outside, the only sound was of the tree limbs cracking with frost. Génie and the others grew such heavy coats that they looked more like woolly bears than horses. Half a dozen times a day Pierre, François and Jean-Luc took it in turns to check on them, replenishing their hay and chopping away the layer of ice that rimed the water trough. Piles of manure stained the snow outside the barn. For months it went on, until gradually the cold eased, the snow melted and the river began to flow again.

The twentieth of May came and went. Génie's foal was expected at any time, and Pierre was sleeping on a hay bale, getting up two and three times in the night to light his lantern and check her paddock. After a long winter in the barn, the other horses were happy to be back outside in the grassy fields, but as each mare's time grew close, she would be brought in to the safety of a paddock near the stable.

The twenty-fifth of May, and still Génie's foal was not born. A cold lump of fear started to grow in Pierre's belly.

Something was wrong. Génie was huge; her breathing was laboured. Something was very wrong. Pierre felt the familiar weight of guilt descend again. He should have left her in France, he berated himself, in the elegant stables attached to the palace. He should never have brought her here, to this wilderness. He had risked her life for a dream, his dream, and now it looked as though both the dream and the horse might die.

Pierre closed his eyes and prayed, though he feared what God's answer might be. After all, Génie was not his horse. He had stolen her out from under the nose of the King! The fact that he loved her might make no difference. Then again, he believed, it might.

"Please, princess, you'll be all right. Please, God, make it so." Over and over, Pierre muttered the words, willing Génie to be strong.

The dark hours passed slowly. In the night silence, Pierre could hear the beating of his own heart. Above it, suddenly, he heard a low sound, a grunt of effort, a shuffle of straw. Holding his lantern aloft, he moved softly toward Génie's paddock. She was pacing heavily up and down, up and down, swishing her tail and twisting her head to look at her flanks. Pierre smiled. Finally, it was beginning. He settled himself quietly beside the fence to wait, all his earlier fears forgotten. Génie was young and strong and healthy; it was unlikely that she would need any help from him.

The first streaks of dawn were just beginning to lighten

the darkness when the mare's waters broke and Pierre saw the foal's forefeet appear, still covered with membrane. Génie got awkwardly to her feet as though to stretch her legs, took a mouthful of hay and lay down again, waiting for the next contraction. The foal's head appeared, lying on its upper forelegs, then its shoulders and then with a rush, the rest of its body. Génie whinnied softly in delight as she took stock of her baby, and Pierre grinned from ear to ear. He knew better than to interfere at this moment. Instinct would tell the mare what to do. Pierre watched as Génie began to lick the foal, nuzzling encouragement as it struggled to find its feet. By heaven, thought Pierre exultantly, it's a colt. The first one born on North American soil. He murmured a brief prayer of thanks as he sat in the straw and dreamed of a future where the offspring of Génie's colt would help his countrymen plough and haul and settle the land. In his mind's eye, he saw a breed of horse evolving that would be renowned for its pluck, its vigour and its strong constitution: a little iron horse.

The Bear Tree

◦— by Victoria Miles

Bumps in the mattress poke bruises into my back and the bed smells sour and stale. It will only get worse in the months before there is fresh straw again. I am not sure how long I have before dawn, but I must not move or make a sound. I will not be the one who makes this day begin.

My older sister Jacqueline has one side of the bed, Marie, who is ten, is on the other. I lie, stiff and straight, in the middle. The boys, Adrien, Étienne and Jean, share another lumpy mattress next to us, and our parents have theirs against the back wall. If I were to cough, I would probably wake them all, so close are we in this one room, except perhaps for Jean who always sleeps as if he were a new baby — though he turned eight in January.

Trapped in the bed between my sleeping sisters, there is nothing to do in the dark quiet but think back to the day that changed everything for me. The day Jean Aubuchon stepped out of his canoe and onto the riverbank below our farm.

AUGUST 1654

We are all working in the vegetable garden. I am pulling carrots and when I stand up to rest my back, I see a man pulling a canoe onto the riverbank.

"We have a visitor," says Papa and he dusts off his hands to welcome him.

We often have visitors. Papa does some trading for beaver pelts and those who come are welcome to spread their blankets before our hearth for the night.

But this lone man comes empty-handed up to where Papa waits. They speak words I cannot hear and then turn towards the rest of us in the garden. "Marie," says Papa to Maman, "this is Jean Aubuchon." Then he introduces the rest of us. We nod at the man as Papa recites our names. Mine is the last he shares and it seems that "Marguerite" floats in the still, hot air for a long time, before Papa says anything more.

"*Jacqueline est mariée,*" Papa continues and my sister nods again, confirming this is true. "Three years ago. She lives with us still, but she will join her husband on his farm after harvest." Jean Aubuchon frowns slightly at this and I am not surprised. It is so obvious. He is not the first man to have come here looking for a wife. And Jacqueline is very strong. She is taller even than my Papa. Every summer her shoulders grow broader from helping Papa clear trees to make the farm spread further back from the river. When Jacqueline was twelve, Maman stopped working in the woods altogether. Papa talks often of how sorry he will be when Jacqueline must leave to join her husband. He says it will be a great loss to our growing farm.

I think that will be the end of it then, since Papa has made it clear Jacqueline is not available. I expect this man will turn back to his canoe, like the others who have been here before him. Instead, Papa offers him a drink from the jug we share and invites him to rest on the doorstep of our house. Jean Aubuchon accepts, and I watch as rivulets of cider run down his moustache and through his long, dark beard. His hair is held back from his face with a thin strip of leather — the way I wear mine. Two cider stains spread on his shirt, which is so dirty I am not sure of its true colour, and the cloth clings to his back with sweat.

"You must stay for supper," says Papa cheerfully. "Marguerite will stew some eel for us. She is becoming a fine cook." I am uncertain of why he has said this and I do not like the attention. It is rare, coming from Papa.

Jean Aubuchon stays for supper. At the table he speaks only to Maman and Papa. But twice when I look up, I find him staring at me. After we eat, he and Papa wander outside and Papa shows him the farmyard. I cannot hear what they say to each other, nor do I wish to.

Jean Aubuchon stays the night, and the next one, and the night after. Each day he helps Papa and Jacqueline in the forest, cutting down trees. All three of them stink of the bear grease they wear, to keep the flies from biting while they work, but to me, Jean Aubuchon smells the worst. Like a stranger. When we gather around the table, he boasts of his fur trading, and the blankets and axes he has exchanged to pile his canoe full of beaver pelts.

It is Jacqueline who finally tells me why he is here. Why he did not leave that first day.

"They talked in the woods today. He wants to marry you," she whispers to me in bed on the third night of Jean Aubuchon's stay. My throat tightens, but before I can say anything, Maman tells us to be quiet and go to sleep. Jacqueline rolls onto her side without another word, and I am left to lie here, in the hot, stuffy room with the true reason of Jean Aubuchon's presence to keep me awake.

At breakfast, I cannot look at Jean Aubuchon. He does not seem to notice, but announces, to no one in particular, that he will be leaving today. I feel relieved. No one has said anything about a marriage. Could I only have imagined what Jacqueline said last night?

Before he leaves Jean Aubuchon gives presents to all of us. For my father, three bottles of wine from France. There is a bolt of soft wool cloth for Maman. The boys are handed hunting knives while Jacqueline asks for an axe. Marie chooses a packet of ribbons. I do not touch his presents. I feel sick at the thought of taking anything from him. I shake my head at the ribbons, and turn away when he offers me more of the cloth like Maman's. "Don't be a fool; stop being so rude," hisses Maman in my ear. But I cannot obey her. I cannot welcome him, or his gifts. Marie asks Jean Aubuchon if she may have my ribbons and squeals happily when he says yes.

As he pushes away from the bank in his canoe, I realize this stranger did not once speak to me in the days he was here. Maman has me wait as the others turn back to the house, and then she tells me what Papa and Jean Aubuchon have decided.

"It is true, Marguerite, what Jacqueline said last night. He wants to marry you," says Maman. I look down at my bare feet, and feel the tears come up into my eyes. I start to turn away from her, but she grabs my arm and makes me look at her.

"*C'est important, Marguerite.* You must listen. Your Papa has agreed."

And then it comes out of me, all at once, what I have been thinking, since Jean Aubuchon first turned his eyes from Jacqueline to me.

"*Non, non, non!*" I cry, and shake myself free. "I cannot marry him! I am too young! I do not like him! I do not *know* him! *We* do not know him! How can you say this? How can you think it?"

"It's been decided," says Maman. "I know you are young, but you must accept it. Your Papa has given his word." She looks very tired, and old, but also very serious.

"But why, Maman, why now? It's too soon! Why can't I wait?"

She tries to reason with me. "Think, Marguerite. Monsieur Aubuchon is a young man. He has some land. He has ambition. He told Papa he will be a merchant soon, from the fur trade. And he has given your Papa his promise. He will not quit this place, he will not return to France, so long as he has a wife. Other men will come — and they may be older. Much older. Was Madame de Champlain not a young bride?"

She seems satisfied by her reasoning. But I am not.

"He only wants me to help clear his farm!" I argue. No one ever argues with Maman. But this time, I cannot stop myself. "He should hire men if he wants help! Or buy a pair of oxen! Or marry a woman his own age!" I am crying hard now, and twisting away from Maman. But she only grasps my arm more tightly.

She changes her tone. Consoling. Kinder. "You don't have to marry him tomorrow. Not until after your birthday, and that is some time away, is it not? And Papa has said you will stay with us for at least two years after that. Just as was agreed for Jacqueline."

In her eyes I can see that already I have spent her little patience for me. She lets me go and I whirl and run. I am the smallest in my family, and though my feet are bare, when I run I do not feel the ground. I leave Maman standing on the riverbank, and I do not look back.

I run past the barn and the house. My little brother Jean is in the pig pen, pouring slops. He calls to me, "Marguerite, what has happened?" but I do not stop to answer. I race over the path we have worn through the wheat field and into the meadow where the cows and the oxen graze.

At the edge of the forest I stop and gulp the air. It is cooler here, and I push from my mind the Iroquois danger. The forest is never a place to be alone, but in this moment I do not care. I lift my skirt, wipe my face and when I am steady again, I weave through shafts of sunlight and dusky shadows to a tree Papa and I found together when I was very small. All the trees on our land seemed gigantic to me then, but this one pine, which towers over its neighbours, was easily twice the width of any other tree in the forest. Even Papa was impressed. He had a look on his face that I saw only once before, when petit Jean was born. I didn't understand it then, but now I know it was awe.

"This must be the place where the bear died," said Papa softly.

"Bear, what bear, Papa?" It was confusing, the way he said it. As if there were bear bones curled up in the ground beneath our feet. Every fall, Papa would hunt for bear. If he killed one, he would build a travois and bring an ox to drag it home. He always waited until autumn, as close to the first snowfall as he could suppose, when the bears were at their fattest. The bigger the bear, the brighter our winter, Papa always said, for we burned bear grease in lamps when the days were short and dark. The smell was foul, but it was better, we thought, than going to bed early.

"Papa, what bear?" I tugged his sleeve, begging him to explain.

He crouched down and stroked a tree root thicker than his arm. "In a place where something wild dies, and its body remains, the earth is the richer for it," he said and stood up. He seemed to lose interest then. "Really," he shrugged, "it is just an old saying."

That is all Papa ever said about the bear tree, and the only time we visited it together. I think he has forgotten it by now. When petit Jean was four or five, I took him to find the tree. When we found it, his face was the same as Papa's. *"C'est incroyable!"* Jean said excitedly. Incredible. I had never heard him use that word before. "We could dig out a cave in the trunk, and live inside!"

"Non, non Jean, cet arbre m'est très cher." We mustn't do anything to it. Papa says it is the place where the bear died." Jean's eyes became rounder when he heard this and his mouth silently formed the words, to say them back to himself: "the place where the bear died."

Today it is not so hard to find the bear tree. The farm creeps closer upon it every year. When I lean against the trunk and look back in the direction of the river, I can see where the clearing meets the woods. I worry what will happen to this tree when Papa and his axe arrive.

I slump down into the soft duff and lean back against the tree. I am too tired from running to cry anymore. All I want to do is sit and wish grimly for cruel waters to meet Jean Aubuchon and his canoe.

The forest has a quiet floor, and my brother's voice finds me before his footsteps tell me he is here. "Marguerite?"

I do not answer, though I know he means well by following me, and I should be glad. When Jean was very young, the croup caught him one winter, and would not let him go. Papa plugged every draughty crack in the house with mud from the barn floor and Maman stretched the leather parchment tighter across the windows, to keep the cold from slipping inside.

It was most terrible at night; his gasping for breath — a sharp slicing sound — took in only a sliver of air at a time. One night his lips turned blue as he struggled to breathe, and I feared we would lose him. Three days passed. Maman took sick as well, so I did what she told me for Jean while she rested. I warmed a cloth near the fire, smeared goose fat on it, and laid it on his chest. I boiled water and sat him before it, his head covered in a linen sheet to keep the steam from escaping. And I held his head and coaxed him to sip hot mint tea. All this lasted, night and day, for almost a week, but finally petit Jean could rest and breathe easily once again.

Ever since, my little brother has been more dear to me

than anyone else in my family. He is the only one to whom I have ever shown the bear tree, so he knows it is the place to find me when no one else can.

Jean sits down beside me. "You have to marry him, don't you?"

I shake my head, but my voice betrays my will. "Yes, Papa has decided it."

Jean sits very still. "I will miss you, when you have to go." He looks at me so honestly when he says this that I almost start to cry again. I give him a hug, which I have not done for a long time, as he doesn't like to hug anyone, anymore. He doesn't like to be the baby, to be teased by Étienne and Adrien for being the youngest. He was very proud the day Papa gave him the job of pig-keeper and he strutted around the farm for days afterward, full of importance. Today, he hugs me back.

"I can't stay, I left the pigs loose," Jean says. "They'll be everywhere now." He stands up. "If Papa sees . . ." he makes a face, and I stand up too.

"Then we'll just have to find them before he does." We hurry back to the farm together, and as we whistle and call and chase the pigs back into their pen, I forget my fate . . . for a little while.

All that was last August. Sealed away by a winter that has just begun to thaw. Now I lie in the quiet, a few moments longer, before sunrise warms the hide that covers the window above my parents' bed. Soft light glows through the oiled deerskin, just enough to wake my mother. The day begins and, for all I have tried to keep still, I must be part of it.

Neighbours will come to the house, and they will celebrate my wedding. A fiddler will come from another farm and there will be dancing. We must cook for more people than our barn can hold.

After the dishes are cleared away, Maman begins to give directions. Then she joins me in the cellar and we pick through the carrots, turnips and cabbages to find the best of what remains from last year's store. Everything is soft and wrinkly by now, but there is still enough to see us through spring. We fill our aprons and return to the kitchen.

"I wish there were some flowers for today, something blooming in the garden." Her voice sounds cheerful, but when I glance at her, her face looks sad and there are dark shadows under her eyes. "I had a bouquet of primroses on my wedding day and violets in my hair. But that was in France," she sighs and brushes sand off the parsnip in her hand. "April here," she frowns, "it is always too soon for flowers."

All I hear is "too soon". The words stay with me all morning. They travel with me in my head as we trudge through slush, following Papa, to the chapel. We are all together, except for petit Jean, who disappeared before we left the house. It would not be hard to find him, if someone chose to sort out the confusion of footprints in the mud and snow in the farmyard. But Papa says there is no time, we have made Monsieur Aubuchon wait long enough.

As we reach the chapel, a voice calls me to look back.

"Arrêtes Marguerite! Arrêtes!" petit Jean cries and charges through wet snow. In his hand he is clutching a long bundle — pussywillows. "For you," he says proudly, and thrusts them into my empty hands.

I cannot speak to thank him, but turn towards the chapel, where the priest and Jean Aubuchon wait inside. As Papa pushes open the door, I mark this last moment, when I am still Marguerite Sédilot. I will leave here today Marguerite Aubuchon. And I will be, as I was when I awoke this morning, twelve years and eight days old.

AUGUST, 1660

Every morning now, my nightdress and the bed beneath me are soaked with my perspiration, so much so that Marie refuses to sleep beside me any longer, and has taken, for her bed, a bearskin on the floor. My husband brought me back to Maman and Papa a month ago. He left for our farm again the next day, saying he will not be back until the baby is born.

I am the last to rise and dress, the slowest at breakfast, reluctant to move from the table, though everyone else is done. I sit there and look at my hands, red and swollen, and wait for Maman to order me in the direction of a chore.

But for once I am spared. Instead she says, "Walk, walk, it is good to walk. Walk, and perhaps it will bring on the baby."

"Jean," she calls out from the front door. "Go with your sister, make her *walk.*" Maman pushes me gently up from the bench and outside.

"Come this way," says Jean, softly in the deep voice that always sounds so strange to me now, as if it is someone else speaking. I was not here when Papa's voice became my brother's, too. "There's something you must see." We walk the path to the woods. The sun is so bright, I follow my brother's lead, looking down at my belly the whole way, for I cannot see my feet any longer. This day is too hot for walking, I complain. I am very slow, and I want to turn back. But Jean is patient, just a little further, he says, not far.

"What will you call the baby, if it is a boy?" Jean asks.

"Médéric."

"And if it is a girl?"

"I do not know," I say in a dull voice. "Perhaps Marie."

And then somehow, with so few words traded between us, we step suddenly out of the sun and into a circle of shade. "There you are," says Jean and he is smiling. "Papa would not let us cut it. He said it is yours."

It is greater still than I remember, tall and wide over me — the tree where the bear died. All around us the forest is gone, the field an ugly rubble of stumps and shrubbery and felled trees. But against this one left standing I lean and inhale the fresh scent of pine. Jean helps me to sit. At last I rest my back against the bear tree and take strength for all the work there will be in my life, and all the children and all the years still to come.

Farewell the Mohawk Valley

๑— by Jean Rae Baxter

Charlotte and her father finished the milking. Then he carried the full pails into the milk shed while she spread fodder on the ground for the cattle. The cows' bells jangled as they fed. Charlotte heard the clanking of pails from the milk shed. In a few minutes her father came out.

"Before it gets dark, I'm going to ride over to Herkimer's place to see if he wants to buy the cattle. I'll try to sell him the pigs too." Papa stood looking at her, but she did not answer. "Tell your mother."

"Please, Papa, tell her yourself. It will break Mama's heart if we have to leave the valley."

"The rebels are going to drive us out anyway. Might as well get something for the livestock if we can."

"I can't bear to tell her." Charlotte glanced towards the house, and there was Mama standing at the window watching them. She looked as if she was marked off into little squares by the panes of window glass. With the light of the fire behind her, Mama's red hair was the colour of flame.

"You're right," Papa said softly. He was looking at Mama. "I'll tell her myself when I get back. Ask her to keep my supper warm." It was not yet dark, though the sun had set. Papa had five miles to ride, then five miles to ride back. The moon would be up before he got home. Charlotte finished foddering the cattle, then let them into the barn. Even though it was still October, this was going to be a cold night.

Mama had set the table with three places. Papa's place was at the end, with Charlotte's place on his left and her mother's on his right. The whole other end of the long table looked bare and empty without places set for the boys. The room, too, felt empty without Charlotte's three brothers joking and whistling and shoving each other around.

Charlotte and her father had butchered a pig the day before, and the lovely smell of roasting meat filled the room. But Charlotte barely glanced at the roast turning on the spit as she hurried by. "Papa wants you to keep his supper warm for him," was all she said. She tried to slip up the stairs to avoid any questions. Mama stopped her.

"Why is your father galloping off down the road with supper all ready?"

"He has to see Mr. Herkimer about something."

Mama opened her mouth as if about to speak, then stopped. Charlotte figured that her mother already knew. "We'll wait supper till he gets back," Mama said.

Charlotte went upstairs to change her gown and brush her hair. She had a bedroom to herself because she was the only girl, although for the past year she had not felt much like a girl, or lived a girl's life. With her brothers gone, she had to help bring in the hay, milk the cows, slaughter pigs and chop wood just like a man.

There was a framed hole in the floor of Charlotte's bedroom, as in all the bedrooms, to allow warmth to rise to the upper storey. Noise also rose, so that nothing happening downstairs was secret from anyone upstairs.

After she had changed her gown and tidied her hair, Charlotte lit a candle and lay down on her bed to read until Papa returned. By remaining upstairs she could avoid Mama's worried face. She listened for the snick of the door latch, and when she heard it, she put down her book. Papa was home. As soon as the door closed, she heard her mother say, "You went down there to sell the animals, didn't you?"

"Yes, I tried. But Herkimer wasn't buying. He hinted that before long they'd be confiscated anyway. If he waits, he reckons he can get our livestock dirt cheap." Charlotte heard the thump of her father's boots hitting the floor, first one then the other, and a heavy sigh as he sat down. "We're regarded as outlaws, Martha. If people steal our goods and burn our house, the law will not protect us. One of these days the Sons of Liberty will pay us a visit, and then we'll be lucky if we're even left alive."

Mama was starting to cry. "Henry, I don't want to leave."

"I know, dearest. But we must."

"How will Isaac find us if we're gone when he comes back?"

"He'll find us. We'll go north to one of the British forts. Isaac will seek us there. He's a sensible young man. If we aren't with the refugees at one fort, he'll try another. Never fear."

"No, Henry. We must not leave until Isaac comes home." Mama means it, Charlotte thought.

Isaac was the youngest of the brothers. All three had gone to fight for the British and had been with General Burgoyne at Saratoga. James and Charlie were dead, their bodies recovered from the battlefield. But Isaac's body was not among them. Where was Isaac? He might be in Boston, where a remnant of the beaten British force was imprisoned. Or he might have escaped. Indians had been fighting on the British side. Some got away, following forest trails known only to them. Isaac might have escaped with the Indians. Even now he could be making his way home. General Burgoyne had surrendered on October 17th, a week ago. It was barely a three-day journey from Saratoga, even through the bush. This very night there might be a rap at the door, and Mama would rush to let him in; for she always slept downstairs now, in constant readiness for his return.

"Please, God, let Isaac come home," Charlotte whispered. She stood up and smoothed her gown. It was time to go downstairs and help Mama serve supper.

Papa hardly noticed Charlotte entering the room, though he usually looked at her with a smile when she appeared with her hair dressed, wearing a fresh gown. Papa did not like to see her skirts trailing in the mud or stained with barnyard manure. But when all three boys went off in the same week to join the King's New York Royal Rangers, it was Papa who had said, "Well, Charlotte, I reckon you'll have to put away your knitting and help me run the farm."

Charlotte did not complain. At fifteen, she knew her duty and was proud to do it. She was strong and tall — her father's child, with the same big frame, brown eyes and black, curly hair (though Henry's was grizzled now). Solid as a rock, people said.

In no point of appearance did Charlotte resemble her brothers. Most people found it difficult to tell one Hooper brother from another, though the three taken together, with their flaming red hair and freckled skin, looked different from anyone else in the Mohawk Valley — except their mother. They had the same hair, the same lightly built frame. They were Martha's boys, flesh and bone, body and soul.

The boys were all fire and air — quick to ignite and fast

to burn. They had taken the King's shilling before the ink was scarce dry on the American Declaration of Independence, never stopping to think how Papa would manage with all of them gone. But how brave they had looked in their scarlet coats! Charlotte had hugged them and wondered whether she would ever see her handsome brothers again.

The boys had always been Charlotte's heroes. They had seemed so exciting when she was still a little girl. She remembered how they used to arrive home from school together, bursting into the house like a whirlwind — all fists and freckles, shouts and rude jokes — while she sat playing with her doll in the chimney corner. Little sister.

Martha and Henry had married late. Martha had not been intended for marriage, being expected, as her parents' youngest daughter, to remain single to care for them in their old age. But by the time she was thirty, both her parents had died, leaving her free. Henry courted quickly. Three red-headed boys were born in as many years. Then five years passed before Martha conceived one last time, giving birth to Charlotte, her only daughter.

The family ate supper in silence, all three seated at one end of the trestle table that should have held twice that number. After they had eaten, Papa had more news to relate. "I passed by the church in Fort Hunter," he said. "There was singing and shouting inside that did not sound like a joyful noise unto the Lord. I stopped my horse and went to the door. My dears, they have turned our church into a tavern. The scoundrels had a barrel of rum set upon the reading desk. I looked, then rode away."

"You were lucky they didn't stop you," said Charlotte. "There's no telling what they might have done."

"Reverend Stuart has angered every Whig in the valley," said Martha. "In his sermons he preaches loyalty to the Crown. He never omits Prayers for the King, however much he is mocked. Now it seems that he has lost his church. I wonder what will happen to him and his family now."

"They'll not come to harm," said Henry. "John Stuart is too much respected by people in high places. But plain folks like us are not safe. We should have left a year ago when Sir John Johnson asked us to join his group. We would all be in Montreal by now."

"Not the boys," said Martha.

"No. Not the boys," said Henry. "They were bound to go for soldiers. Not even you could have stopped them, Martha."

"I wouldn't have tried."

"What are we going to do?" Charlotte asked. "Will you try to sell the animals in town?"

"No, daughter. We'll put them out in the cow pasture and leave them. Forget about the animals. We have no choice. We must leave now, while we can. All the way back from Herkimer's I thought it over. Tomorrow I want you and your mother to do some sewing."

"Sewing?" Charlotte asked.

"Yes. Take the money we have, and your rings and brooches, and any other small things that are valuable, and stitch them into your petticoats.

"I have a strongbox for our papers and a piece of canvas to wrap the silver tea set my parents brought from England. I'll bury everything down by the rock pile the boys made when we cleared the back acre for potatoes. Anyone going by will think I'm just spading the last of the potatoes. After the war is over, Isaac and I will come back to dig up the box and silver. Even if we lose the farm, we'll find a way to recover things buried in the earth."

The next day was blustery, with cold rain lashing the windows. Charlotte and her mother sat by the fire and sewed. Each took two petticoats and, placing one inside the other, quilted them together. But the only pattern to their quilting was that determined by the shape of the objects stitched up inside. There were coins and pound notes, rings and brooches, silver spoons, even Henry's gold pocket watch and chain. There was a silver locket, too, which a boy named Nick Schyler had given to Charlotte. She had been his sweetheart — before Tory meant Loyalist and friend, and Whig meant Rebel and foe.

Throughout the long, rainy day Charlotte and her mother sewed. From time to time Charlotte stood up and, holding the double petticoat by its waistband, tested the weight. Finally Charlotte said, "This is enough. I shan't be able to walk if my petticoats are weighted with one more thing."

Mama went to the window. She looked out over the fields which her men had cleared of stumps and stones, over the snake fence that zigzagged between orchard and cow pasture, and all the way to the dark forest beyond. She's thinking about Isaac, Charlotte supposed. She's wondering if he is out there in the bush, trying to make his way home.

Charlotte took her mother's arm and gently drew her away from the window. "He's not out there, Mama."

Mama answered in her lowest voice, "I cannot leave until Isaac has come home."

In the morning Papa buried his strongbox and the silver. Then he saddled his horse and rode off in the direction of Fort Hunter. He was gone most of the day. When he returned, he was on foot. "I gave my horse to Reverend Stuart," he said, and pulled three guineas from his pocket. "This is his thanks." From another pocket he drew out a folded sheet of paper. "He gave me a map, too," he said, and spread it on the table. It was crudely hand-drawn — more a sketch than a map. Charlotte and her mother stood beside him as he traced the route which they would follow. Here was their home. There the Mohawk River with its western branch leading towards Oneida Lake. They must cross Oneida Lake, then follow the Oswego River to its mouth. He rested his finger on the spot where Lake Ontario flows into the St. Lawrence River. "Carleton Island lies here. It is well fortified, with a strong garrison and good provision for refugees. We shall stay the winter there."

"There are no towns along the way!" exclaimed Martha. "Only wilderness!"

"Martha, do you think it would be safer for us to go through towns? The Sons of Liberty are everywhere. You don't know the things they have done to Loyalists in the last few months. Men tarred and feathered. Women subjected to the most terrible, unspeakable insult."

Charlotte knew what that meant. In 1777 a Loyalist girl was fair game for any Liberty man. She didn't want to think about that. Yet if they had to make their way through the woods, there would be other problems. "How can Mama and I walk through the bush in long gowns?" she asked.

"We'll follow Indian trails," he said. "One of Reverend Stuart's Mohawk friends marked them on this map. When we reach Oneida Lake, Mohawk guides will meet us with a long canoe. They'll take us the rest of the way. It is all arranged."

"You got good value for that horse," said Martha.

When Charlotte woke the next morning, the room was still dark. She snuggled deep into the feather mattress and pulled the quilts over her head. Curled up in this womb of warmth, she wondered how long it would be before she slept in a bed again. She thought about Nick and wondered how often he thought about her, now that the war had driven them apart. Once there had been sweet kisses, and he had carved their initials into the bark of a sycamore tree.

She could hear Mama already busy downstairs. It was time to get up — time for the day of departure to begin.

After her chores, Charlotte walked across the field where Henry had buried the strongbox and silver. Spade marks and boot marks could still be seen in the soft soil by the rock pile. She climbed over the snake fence and struck into the woods, picking up the familiar pathway that led to the ravine. In ten minutes she reached the great sycamore on the crest.

There was the heart that Nick had carved on the tree's grey trunk with their initials C.H. and N.S. entwined. With her fingers she traced the shape of the heart, and kissed it. Dear Nick. She would never sit with him again under this tree, looking out over the lovely valley.

Below, down the steep slope, were cedars and hemlocks, white birches and dark pines. At the bottom of the ravine a little brown snake of a creek wound its way. Under the overcast sky, everything was shadowed and dim.

Then she saw the splash of red amongst the trees below. It looked like a daub of scarlet paint, brighter than blood.

Charlotte could not take her eyes from the red. Fear stopped her breath. She stood with her back braced against the sycamore, her open palms pressed against the smooth bark. Then, slowly, her legs began to move, and she clambered down the steep slope faster and faster, grasping at roots, stems, branches. For a minute, trees hid the red from her sight, then she saw it again. Near the bottom she ran and fell, then ran again. She pushed through bushes, brambles catching at her clothes and twigs at her hair. At the edge of the tree line she paused, too afraid for a moment to face what might lie ahead. She had to force herself to take the last few steps.

When she entered the clearing there was no sound, no motion, only a soldier lying on the scuffed carpet of pine needles and dry leaves. Above the scarlet coat was her brother's pale, freckled face, and on his face an expression of faint surprise. His blood-soaked hair was dark as mahogany. Charlotte knelt beside him and touched his cold cheek. With her fingertips she separated the sticky strands of his matted hair and saw the small, round hole where the bullet had entered. Then she closed his eyes. Well, Isaac, she thought, you almost made it back. What a target that red coat must have been for any rebel skulking in these woods!

Then a cold feeling ran through her. One of our neighbours killed him, she thought. Someone we know took Isaac's life. Tears of grief and rage and despair ran down her cheeks. Charlotte stood up. Still looking at Isaac, she slowly backed away and returned to the shelter of the trees.

Her eyes were almost blinded with tears as she climbed the hill. She tried to think of the words she would have to say when she got home, but it was no use. Charlotte climbed over the snake fence, and her legs carried her across the fields to the farmhouse. She paused for a moment in front of the door, then pressed the latch and went in.

Mama turned pale when she saw Charlotte's face. "What happened to you?" Her voice was low and her lips trembled, as if she were ready for any kind of horror. For a moment Charlotte could not speak, but stood with jaws clenched.

Papa said nothing. His eyes met Charlotte's above Mama's head, and he nodded his head in an odd circular motion that included both "yes" and "no" in a gesture of understanding. Then, taking a step forward, he put one arm around Mama's shoulder. Charlotte ran to them from across the room. They clung to one another, all three weeping. Mama was shaking so hard that she might have fallen to the floor if Charlotte and Papa had not been holding her tightly.

They went together to the ravine. Papa carried Isaac home across his shoulders. He dug a grave for him in the orchard. Mama brought her best quilt to wrap his body. Charlotte nailed two sticks together to make a cross. Then they went back to the house.

"We can leave now," said Mama. "Isaac has come home."

Rule of Silence

∽ by Ann Walsh

The warden of the Provincial Penitentiary of Upper Canada was asleep when the prisoners were brought before him. His head rested on the Punishment Book, open on his desk. He snored gently. A small spot of spittle blotted an entry in the book smudging the description, written yesterday, of one the offences. "November 6, 1845, prisoner leaving work and going to the outhouse without permission."

The warden snored. The prisoners shuffled. The guard coughed softly, then again, louder this time.

Slowly the warden lifted his head, leaning back in his chair. He looked at the Punishment Book, blinked, then wiped at the page with his sleeve. "Yes? What is it?" he asked, his voice thick with sleep.

"The new prisoners, sir," said the guard. "You wanted to see them before they go to their cells."

"Of course, of course," said the warden, still dabbing at the smudged page. "These will be the famous pickpockets."

"Famous, sir?"

The warden studied the smeared page. The words telling of the offence that had been committed were fainter now. But the words describing the punishment given to the prisoner — "six lashes with cat-o'-nine-tails" — were still clear and easy to read. The warden sighed with relief. The records were intact; no one would ever know that the Punishment Book had been sullied. Perhaps no one would ever notice the stain; hopefully no one would ever know what had caused it.

"A journalist from Lower Canada wrote about these prisoners in *The Montreal Gazette* last month," he explained to the guard, closing the Punishment Book as he spoke. "'Old offenders', that's what the newspaper called them. Old offenders, indeed." He smiled. "They'll grow older before their sentences have been served in my penitentiary. Much older." Then he lifted his head and, for the first time, looked directly at the prisoners.

He saw a tall bearded youth and two others, one dark haired, one blonde, both shorter and clean shaven. "One, two, three," he counted aloud. "There were to be *four*. Where is the other one?"

"Here, sir," said the guard. "Right here." He pointed, but

the warden still saw nothing.

"Where?" he asked, pushing himself up in his chair and peering over the top of his high desk. A very small boy stood directly in front of him, so close that only the top of his head was visible. "Stand up, young man," demanded the warden. "Let me see your face, not just your unkempt hair."

The boy straightened, but even then his head scarcely cleared the top of the warden's desk. There was silence for a moment as the warden stared. Something about the child's wide eyes, his tousled hair and the smudge of dirt on his cheek prompted the warden to say, "So. You must be Oliver."

The guard looked at the papers in his hand. "No, sir. He is Antoine. Antoine Beauché."

"I was making a literary reference," said the warden, settling back in his chair. "My wife, a most cultured woman, has been reading aloud a book by Mr. Dickens of England. That type of sensational work is not my choice in literature, but you know how wives are. Every night she reads; every night I must listen. Although I am a most compassionate man, I find this story unbelievable. The author writes *sympathetically* about young criminals, offering reasons — such as poverty — to excuse their wickedness. Mr. Dickens tries to makes the reader feel sorry for his hero, Oliver, who is nothing more than a thief."

"Sir?"

The guard had not understood. Again the warden

explained. "The novel my wife is reading aloud. The book by Mr. Dickens. It is about a young boy named Oliver Twist, a pickpocket and a most devious child."

"Oh, books!" said the guard. "I don't read 'em."

That fact did not surprise the warden. He turned his attention back to the prisoners. "Move away from the desk, young Oliver," he said. "Stand where I can see you."

One of the boys spoke. "Sir, Antoine *ne comprend pas* — he does not understand the English." He reached out a hand, pulling the smallest boy to him. There was a resemblance between the two children, thought the warden. Ah, he remembered now. Some of this gang were brothers.

The warden smiled magnanimously. "Well, young Oliver, if you have no English, you may answer me in French. I am exceptionally fluent in French — and in Latin and German as well. How old are you, boy?"

There was no answer.

"Speak, prisoner!"

The older boy, fair haired like Antoine, answered. "Antoine is my brother, sir. He does not understand the English; he understands only français. But he does not speak, not any language. Sometimes he tries, but he makes only small noises. Not words."

"Then I give you permission to talk for him. His age?"

"*Huit ans.* Pardon. Eight years, sir."

"Eight? I believe that gives him the honour of being the youngest of our inmates," said the warden. "The law says that the age of knowing right from wrong is five years old — even though some lenient judges nowadays place that age as high as seven. This child is old enough to know very well that stealing is sinful."

He stared curiously at the boy before turning again to Antoine's brother. "How old are you, young man?"

"*J'ai* — I have twelve years."

"The other shorter prisoner is also twelve," said the guard. "But the tall one, this bearded ruffian is nineteen."

"Mr. Fagin, I presume," said the warden. "The ringleader."

"Who?" asked the guard? He slowly ran his finger down the list of the prisoners' names. "No, sir, the oldest one is called . . . Oh, that must be another one of them literary refusals of yours, sir."

The warden sighed again. "Mr. Fagin is the leader of Oliver Twist's gang of pickpockets in the — "

"Oh, aye sir. I remember. The book your most cultivated wife is reading aloud."

"Mr. Fagin," repeated the warden. "What have you to say for yourself?"

There was no answer. The guard prodded the oldest prisoner. "Speak up, man. He says 'Fagin' but he means you."

"*Moi? Mon nom, ce n'est pas* 'Fagin'."

The guard prodded him again, not gently this time. "If the warden says you are Mr. Fagin, then Mr. Fagin you shall be. Now answer him."

The tall prisoner's eyes narrowed and his lips tightened. "I speak not good the English, monsieur. *Ces enfants* — these children — they steal, many times. Them. Not me. *Je suis innocent.*"

"Of course you are," said the warden. "Amazing how almost all of our prisoners claim to be innocent. Most odd. Well, I have heard enough from you."

"*Non! Je suis innocent.*"

"Silence!" The guard's voice was so loud that even the warden was startled.

"You were asked to be quiet, Mr. Fagin, or whatever your name may be," said the warden sternly.

"*Monsieur, je*—"

"Be quiet!" Now the warden also raised his voice. He would have to make this new prisoner understand. He looked directly at him as he spoke. "Here in the Provincial Penitentiary there is a Rule of Silence which is strictly enforced. This means that you may not talk to another prisoner, to a guard or to me unless asked to do so or necessitated by the performance of your work. You will be silent at *all* times — in your cells, at meals, at your work, during prayers and even in the wash house or the privy. Talking is forbidden because more repenting is done in silence than during idle chatter."

"*Je comprends, monsieur.*"

The warden frowned. "No, you do *not* understand, Mr. Fagin. I did not ask you a question, nor did I give you permission to speak. I specifically said that I had heard enough, yet you continued to talk. As punishment, you shall have only bread and water for supper tonight."

The tall prisoner took a step forward, his eyes angry. The guard yanked him back. He stumbled. But he kept quiet.

Once more the warden turned his attention to the youngest boy. "Why is Oliver holding his leg irons, guard? He is not wearing them. He is not properly secured."

Antoine did not understand, but he saw the warden looking at him and he bowed his head again, clutching the two thick steel anklets, and the chain which connected them, closer to his chest. They were heavy, but he lifted them higher so the chain did not drag. He wished he could put these things on the ground, but his brother had said that he must carry them or the Englishmen would be angry.

"The child's legs are too small, sir. The irons fell off."

"I see. Well, we have restraints for a woman's slender ankles — surely some of those will fit him. Perhaps our Oliver should be housed with the females."

"*Non!* He must be with me. Always Antoine stays with me."

"Silence!" roared the guard again, but Antoine's brother would not be silenced.

"Sir, my brother does not know any parent but me. Since our *mère* . . . mother . . . dies, I am all to him. I look after him. He must not be separated from me."

"You have not listened to me, young man!" said the warden. He was trying to sound calm, but he was becoming angry. "Did I not just explain the Rule of Silence? Did you not understand my words?"

"But sir, Antoine is . . ."

"Bread and water for this one also, guard," said the warden, pointing at Antoine's brother. "For *two* days." He sighed. It disturbed him to punish prisoners so soon after their arrival at his penitentiary, but they must learn to obey.

He explained once more. "Listen carefully. You must never speak unless you are asked to do so. Tonight, when you see your fellow prisoners feasting on boiled cabbage and potato while you gnaw only on a slice of stale bread, then you will remember that if good food is to go into your mouth, no sounds may come out of it."

Antoine was puzzled. What was happening? He shifted the heavy metal objects he held in his arms, wishing again that he could put them down. His brother and friends were wearing these around their ankles, like thick bracelets. There was a short chain between the two "bracelets," and his brother had stumbled when he tried to move quickly. One could not run or skip or jump with those heavy things tying one's ankles together, Antoine thought. He was lucky only to have to carry them, even though they were heavy. He looked at his brother and smiled gratefully.

The warden saw the smile and frowned. What did the child have to smile about, he wondered. "I have seen all I wish to," he said abruptly. "Guard, take the prisoners away.

But watch them carefully. They are devious as well as clever."

"Yes, sir."

"However, perhaps they are not as smart as they think they are," said the warden, laughing. "As I remember, they were arrested because they tried their pickpocket game on a steamship travelling the St. Lawrence River. An alert passenger saw what they were up to; they were easily caught."

"Very easily I imagine, sir," said the guard. "Seeing as how there's no place to escape to, not on a boat. No, sir. Not so de . . . dev . . . clever after all."

"Take this with you," said the warden, handing the guard the Punishment Book. "Remember — one night of bread and water for Mr. Fagin; two nights for Oliver's brother — perhaps he corresponds to the character Mr. Dickens calls the 'Artful Dodger.' Well, whatever else he may be, for the next two days he shall be a hungry dodger."

He watched as the guard led the four away: the ring-leader, Fagin, first, the other twelve-year-old close behind him. Antoine, or "Oliver" as the warden had re-named him, was the last to leave, following his brother. The guard shouted at the prisoners to move quickly; the leg irons shortened their steps, but they shuffled faster.

Except for Antoine. He moved slowly, clutching the shackles in his arms, bent by their weight. For a moment, just as he left the room, he looked back. The warden thought Antoine smiled again, but that could not be so.

Surely the boy realised the severity of his crime; surely he knew of the three long years to which he had been sentenced. There was nothing for the child to smile about.

His stomach rumbled; the warden looked at his watch. It was time for dinner. But first, he must complete his inspection.

Every night he walked through the penitentiary buildings and its grounds, speaking to the guards, checking with the kitchen staff to make sure they had not overspent on food for the next day's meals, making a note of the quantity of limestone brought to the workshop for the prisoners to cut into building blocks. Sometimes he even inspected a cell, although his wife complained when he did, claiming that his clothes smelled dreadfully.

This daily tour pleased the warden. He firmly believed that the Provincial Penitentiary in Kingston, Canada's first penitentiary, only ten years old, was the most up-to-date prison facility in the world.

Young Antoine/Oliver was lucky to be imprisoned *here*, not in a jail where all ages and types of criminals were housed in the same cell, the warden reminded himself. The Provincial Penitentiary's thick limestone walls provided *individual* rooms. These cells were 29 inches across, more than wide enough for the beds, which were hinged so that they could be lifted up against the rear wall during the day. The cells were long enough so that even when the bed was lowered there was nearly two feet of space between its foot and the barred door. And every prisoner had his own covered slop bucket in his cell and was ordered to empty it daily.

Each cell had a large grated window on the rear wall, opening onto an inspection corridor from which the guards could observe the prisoners. Air circulated freely through these windows; proper ventilation was essential to keep prisoners healthy and, the warden reminded himself, healthy prisoners worked much harder than ones who were ill.

The prisoners were given clean clothes, wool trousers and loose shirts, long dresses for the women, coloured yellow down one side and brown down the other. The strange colouring made it easy to identify any convict who escaped and tried to blend into a crowd of honest Kingston citizens. Although made of coarsely woven wool, the clothing was warm and comfortable and was kept clean.

This penitentiary had been built using the most modern designs and technology. Just recently the last section of the high cedar fence which surrounded it had been replaced with thick stone walls; the observation towers were now completed as well, so guards posted there had a clear view of all four of the buildings and the central courtyard.

Good quality limestone, quarried in Kingston, had been used in all the buildings: the three blocks where prisoners were housed and the separate building where the warden, deputy warden and matron lived with their families. The penitentiary also had a prison hospital, a workshop, kitchen, carpentry shop and a garden in which the inmates laboured to provide an inexpensive source of food. Unfortunately, prisoners still needed to be fed, thought the warden. If there were a way to cure them of hunger, the savings would be enormous and the politicians would be most pleased.

Once outside, the warden walked faster, eager for his evening meal. He paused briefly by the prison garden, pulling his long scarf more tightly around his neck. There had been a good crop of potatoes this year, he remembered. Perhaps some had been overlooked when the garden was harvested. He would send a work party to dig in the frozen soil; perhaps the earth would yield a few more vegetables. There was only a light scattering of snow over the garden; the sun touched it every morning and the weather was mild for November — it would be an easy chore. Some of the women could be assigned to take care of it. Or the younger prisoners.

Again he thought of Antoine/Oliver and his gang. By the time they had served their sentences, these boys would have become law abiding citizens who would never again commit a crime. That was the aim of these new penitentiaries, not only to protect society and punish offenders, but to send them back into the world reformed. Unlike common jails where prisoners usually stayed only a short time, waiting for trial and punishments — the stocks, branding, whipping, exile or hanging — penitentiary inmates were allowed the luxury of time to repent.

This reforming of criminals was a sensible idea, the warden believed, although, he thought somewhat regretfully, there seemed to have been fewer hangings recently. But hangings were the responsibility of provincial county jails, not modern penitentiaries such as his. And if the politicians wanted more penitentiaries and fewer hangings — well, he could do nothing about that.

No, young Oliver would not be hanged here. Here he would learn to become a good citizen. He was young, but he would learn. The warden would personally make sure of that. Yes, young Oliver did have a reason to smile, a good reason.

The warden himself smiled all through the evening, even when his wife read aloud from that wretched novel *Oliver Twist*. He was still smiling as he poured himself another small glass of port. It had been a most satisfactory day.

The next morning, the guard brought the Punishment Book for inspection. "How did our two hungry new prisoners manage through the night?" the warden asked.

"They caused no disturbance, sir."

"No, I do not see their names in the book. Good. But here, this is young Oliver, is it not?" Antoine Beauché's name was the last entry on the page, the last record of the rules broken in the night. "Prisoner making noises. Not keeping quiet when told to be silent," the warden read aloud, surprised.

"The child made not a sound when I spoke to him yesterday. In fact, his brother said he did not speak in any language. How, then, did he disturb the peace last night enough for a punishment of . . ." The warden checked the punishment book. "Here it is, yes, 'six lashes, rawhide.'"

"I asked the night watch, sir," said the guard. "It seems that the boy don't speak, but he makes a most fearful racket when he cries."

"He cried?"

"All night they say."

"He wept?"

"Yes, sir. Loudly."

"But yesterday afternoon he was smiling," said the warden.

"That may be, sir, but he did not smile last night."

The warden thought of the cell in which Antoine/Oliver had spent the night. The efficient, modern cell which housed only one prisoner.

"The child is not accustomed to being away from others," he said remembering the older brother's outburst. "I suspect young Oliver has never spent a night alone."

"He'll get used to it," said the guard. "Sooner or later they all get used to it."

The warden stared at the Punishment Book. Since all whippings took place in front of the other prisoners just before the main meal of the day, he knew that Antoine/Oliver had not yet been punished.

Picking up his pen, the warden dipped it carefully in the inkwell. "He is but a child," he said, half to himself. He stared for a while longer at the words "six lashes", then care-fully crossed out the six. "Three will be enough for his first offence," he said making the change to three lashes, rawhide.

Mr. Dickens, he thought, would be pleased.

The First Spike

⌒ by Laura Morgan

I found the diary in an old trunk in the attic of my grandmother's house one lonely Saturday. I had been excluded from a family outing as I had a paper to write for school, and I was seething at the injustice. The topic, "The Last Spike", was too broad and too dull; I could not generate any interest in this supposedly momentous occasion in Canadian history. Our teacher, a Canadiana enthusiast, insisted the Canadian Pacific Railway was the lifeline of Canada, the link that ensured B.C. would forever be married to the union. He avidly read us parts of Pierre Berton's story, and seemed truly inspired by the imagery of that last spike, "the cornerstone of Canadian symbolism." I, however, remained uninspired, and resented being forced to write a paper on a topic that honestly bored me.

After my family drove off, I abandoned my studies in a fit of pique. I wandered through Grandma's house, looking through bookshelves and peeking in drawers. In the attic I discovered the old trunk. Years ago Mother had forbidden me to play with it, as it contained Grandmother's precious things. Picturing jewels and old coins, I creaked open the heavy, dusty lid.

I was disappointed to discover that "precious things" meant no more than old yellowing gloves and handkerchiefs, thick, musty photo albums, crumbly newspaper clippings, ancient baptismal frocks, and, in a bundle of old letters tied with ribbon, the diary.

It was bound in red leather, and it crackled ominously as I opened it, but the ancient binding held. On the inside of the front cover, in a childish hand, was scrawled "Rose Marie Smithson, La Prairie, Lower Canada, 1833." Rose Marie — my own name! I looked again at the date. Over 150 years ago. Long before Grandma — or even Great Grandma — had been born! Eagerly, I turned to the first entry, smudgily inked in the same, irregular hand . . .

SEPTEMBER 17, 1833

Mother says that daily practice shall cure me of the unladylike scrawl that is my shame. I must write in here for half an hour each day. Perhaps if I write very slowly, I will not have to write much at all. This is such a silly exercise. Hopefully Mother will soon forget the whole endeavour.

R. M. S.

SEPTEMBER 18, 1833

Mother read what I wrote last time, and chided me for being saucy. "Even though you are no longer attending school, you must not abandon refinement altogether." I was bold, and told her that I thought memoirs were for one's own confidences, and not to be read by others. (Besides which, I have no intention of ever being ladylike, and although I didn't tell her so, sometimes I feel she puts on airs. Even if she did come from a good family in Boston, she is here in Lower Canada now, and married to a poor smith, so what use do we have of skills like penmanship?) She scolded me, and said "Memoirs indeed! You are only thirteen years old!" But Father stood behind me, and said I was in the right! Victory for me.

R. M. S.

SEPTEMBER 20, 1833

I was correct that Mother would soon forget these penmanship exercises, for she did not remind me yesterday. She was busy with the blueberries we picked. A cousin from Boston wrote her about something called the Appert Process, and mother wanted to try it, as she says it will keep fruit or vegetables fresh all winter without drying them or soaking them in brine. The kitchen is a mess of jars, lids, boiling pots, cooling pots, and such. Matilda and Sue helped her and I was permitted to help Father in the smithy! I am so grimy that I will not mind my bath on Saturday, even if the water is cold!

R. M. S.

I found myself quickly caught up in the world of 1833. Despite her initial protests, Rose Marie continued to add regularly to her "memoirs", and her life seemed fascinating to me. From her entries I gathered that she was an unusual girl for her day — big and strong, eager to learn work that was traditionally masculine in a day and age where it was uncommon for a girl to do heavy labour. I found myself comparing my own time to hers: back then, it was not respectable for a girl to learn anything but "women's work"; in my own time, the term "women's work" was itself disrespectful. I read on . . .

NOVEMBER 6, 1833

Father let me help him in the smithy three days this week. He says to Mother that it is not fair that she has four daughters to help her, when he has no sons to learn his trade. And when I was working the bellows today, a gentleman who was having his horse shod called me "boy" and asked me to fetch him some water! I was wearing an extra apron of father's, and a cap, so I can understand his mistake. Matilda says that she would be mortified, but I think it is rather funny.

R. M. S.

APRIL 9, 1834

I was surprised to come across my "memoirs" on the bookshelf — Mother has long forgotten her project; I expect she has despaired of ever making me ladylike. I am so tall. I am taller even than Mother; I reach up to Father's nose. I like to help in the smithy and Father says I am becoming quite skilled — it's too bad I'm not a boy because I could be his apprentice. Mother is expecting a new babe any day, so maybe he will get his boy.

R. M. S.

MAY 2, 1834

He did! We did! Jacob is so darling, and growing fat, too. We had to sell our milk cow, but Mother will feed him goat milk when he is big enough.

R. M. S.

JANUARY 27, 1835

I am so afraid, and cannot share my fears with anyone. Mother looks worried all the time, and I don't want to frighten my little sisters. Father is sick, and getting worse. I fear he may have the cholera. This winter is terrible cold, and with Father unable to work, we are running short of food.

R. M. S.

MARCH 15, 1835

Father seems better now. He moves slowly, and is very weak, but he is eating more. Jacob is a ray of sunshine to him, and Father talks often of how he will apprentice Jacob when he is older. I had my fifteenth birthday. I am taller than Father, although he pretends to deny it. I am strong and red from helping in the smithy, too. Although Mother doesn't know, I seldom wear my corset — it is so tight, and yet my bodice remains flat. I have to wear Father's old boots; we have no money for new shoes and my feet have grown so. Father lets me wear trousers in the smithy as my skirt gets soiled.

R. M. S.

MAY 22, 1835

I help Father every day now in the smithy. He cannot move well, as the coughing still comes upon him if he does much. I do most of the heavy lifting and hammering. My arms are so strong and thick.

R. M. S

SEPTEMBER 4, 1835

Yesterday, a fellow asked Father if I was his apprentice, and father answered shortly "Family". I believe he is ashamed to have his daughter doing such heavy work. Another fellow said "Yer son is a hard worker" and Father simply replied "Thankee" and winked at me. I would not be other than I am, but I feel comfortable in my trousers and cap, and I feel powerful when I swing a hammer. I am glad I am not small and dainty as Matilda is.

R. M. S.

OCTOBER 11, 1835

Father has been very tired the past few weeks. We don't tell Mother, but often in the smithy he sits on his stool by the fire, and directs me to do the work. He seems in good spirits, but I wish his health would improve.

R. M. S.

DECEMBER 27, 1835

I am numb. I have no one to turn to. Father is dead. Wonderful, warm, laughing Father. How can he be gone? What are we to do?

R. M. S.

JANUARY 11, 1836

Mother is sick with grief. Matilda is holding us together — cooking, and cleaning, and reading to the little ones. Mother wanders like a ghost, and last night she cried to Father in her sleep. Jacob keeps asking for him, and I feel so sad, knowing that Jacob will not remember Father, and that Father will never get to apprentice his beloved son. I wanted to continue working in the smithy, but Mother forbade it. She says I must wear my skirts and find a husband. We have no money at all, and however will we get on? Matilda thinks she can go to work for a seamstress. Her stitches are even and beautiful, but sewing will not support all of us. Mother has asked for help from the cousins in Boston, but nobody will take four children, and we shall have to be split up. And who will want me? I am good for nothing but strong work, and nobody wants a huge girl who looks like a boy and has no prospects.

R. M. S.

FEBRUARY 25, 1836

Today when I brought Matilda her dinner at the seamstress shop, I wore Father's trousers and my old cap. Mother did not see me leave, and I changed in the barn when I returned home. I felt free and invisible in my disguise, and I tipped my hat and whistled and called a gentleman "sir". The seamstress called to Matilda, "Your brother is here with your dinner," and Matilda stared, and covered her giggle with a dainty hand, and winked just as Father used to.

R. M. S.

APRIL 16, 1836

I have been out walking often in my boy costume, and yesterday a man in front of the dry goods store called me over. "Here, you, you look like a big strong fellow. Come help my son unload this wagon. I'll pay you a penny." My arms are still very strong, and we unloaded the wagon quickly; I didn't speak much, so they never knew I was a girl!

R. M. S.

APRIL 23, 1836

I have made a friend. His name is Thomas, and he is the son of the shopkeeper that I helped unload the wagon. Thomas thinks I am a boy. He is seventeen, a year older than I, but because I am so big, he assumed that I was the elder, and I did not correct him. He saw me walking past his father's store, and he asked me my name. I had to think quickly, and said my name was Roman. Thomas likes to talk a lot, and it doesn't seem to bother him that I don't say much. I would like to speak more, but am afraid my voice would give me away. I am unhappy about deceiving him, as he seems a funny and interesting fellow, but to confess now would embarrass us both. He asked me to go fishing tomorrow, and perhaps it is not wise, but I shall think of some excuse to get away.

R. M. S.

MAY 6, 1836

Thomas is a steadfast friend. I told him about Father dying, and the possibility of our family being broken up, and he said he was surprised that a big fellow like me could not find steady work. I hesitated, and said that I was unskilled, and he said "Why, Roman, I believe you are too shy to simply walk up and ask for work." He says he will help me find a job; I don't know what to tell him.

R. M. S.

MAY 10, 1836

Yesterday Thomas and I helped his father with his deliveries. He paid us ten cents each. Thomas says we should look for steady work somewhere.

R. M. S.

MAY 17, 1836

There is talk around town of a railway! Imagine — the first railway in Lower Canada, starting here in La Prairie! The cousins in Boston wrote once about the great locomotives and the tracks that stretch for hundreds of miles! They say the engines pull trains of cars as fast as a team of horses, and that they are very noisy and dirty. Thomas says they will need a gang of strong boys and men to lay the tracks. The pay will be good, and if I am hired on, Mother will not have to ask for help from her Boston relatives. But what will I tell Mother? She would never permit me to disguise myself as a boy.

R. M. S.

MAY 19, 1836

Thomas and I inquired about the railway work, and were hired on at once. I had to tell Matilda. She thinks I am crazy, but as she does not want the family to split up, she is going to help me. I wish we did not have to tell an untruth to Mother, but maybe she will not ask many questions about my "work" in town.

The track will be laid from here to St. Jean, and will be fourteen miles long. The gang has been separated into two groups. One group will work on something called levelling, with wagons and shovels, and one group will lay the track. The crew master put Thomas and me into the latter group. The tracks lie on wooden crosspieces called ties, and great iron spikes must be pounded in. The work starts next week.

R. M. S.

MAY 21, 1836

Mother gave me permission to work in town without much thought at all. She is so sad and distant these days. Matilda says that a cyclone could take the roof off the house and Mother would never even notice. Thomas and I have been talking a lot, and he said something the other day that struck me as funny when I recounted it to Matilda. He said "Roman, for such a big fellow, you really do have a bitty squeaky voice." And I thought I was speaking deeply!

R. M. S.

MAY 25, 1936

We start work tomorrow, at daybreak. I am excited. Matilda is worried that they will find me out once the work starts, but I have wrestled Thomas, and although he beat my right arm, I beat his left. If he is strong enough, I am strong enough. It will be sweaty work though, and I must be careful to bind my chest well, or I will give myself away once my shirt becomes damp!

I am thinking that I will have to tell Thomas of my secret. We spend so much time together that he will surely find out on his own one day. But how can I let him know? Would he be offended, thinking this a joke on him? I fear that it would affect our friendship greatly, and it is a friendship that I hold dear. I find my fondness for Thomas growing daily. He is a fine man, one that anyone would be proud to call friend. How can I chance losing his friendship by confessing? I cannot.

R. M. S.

MAY 26, 1836

My arms are trembling, but I must write a little, although I should not waste the candlelight. Never have I worked as hard as this. We worked from sun-up to sun-down. We stopped once for dinner, and thrice for water. When we arrived, the crew master sent some fellows to lay the ties and tracks, but Thomas and me and some others he set opposite each other, ready to drive the spikes. "You need to strike powerfully," the master said, "using the strength of your legs, back, and arms." He had me drive the first spike, with the others watching. I swung with all my strength. The sledge was heavy, and the spikes are very solid. The blow landed with a sharp, ringing tone that brought suddenly to my mind the image of father shaping a horseshoe. I struck again and again, and each blow reverberated through my arms and back.

At first, we were lighthearted, and made a game of seeing who could drive his spike the fastest. After a while, we concentrated on the work, and by late afternoon we were quite grim. But I did not falter! My arms ache, and I should retire, as tomorrow is coming soon.

R. M. S.

JULY 2, 1836

An odd thing happened during our dinner break today. Thomas clapped his hand on my back, as he has done many times before, but this time it felt odd. I felt the heat of his arm, even after he had removed it, and I felt suddenly awkward. I believe he may have felt my bindings, as he looked at me oddly, and was quiet for the rest of the afternoon.

R. M. S.

JULY 5, 1836

Thomas has indeed discovered my secret. It is Sunday, and so we have no work. He came to call at our house, which he has never done before. I answered his knock myself, expecting a friend of Matilda's. I was wearing my everyday dress. Thomas simply stared, and after a long while, he said "Will you walk with me?"

I am still amazed that he was not angry, but listened quietly to my explanation. At the end of it, he thought for a long time, and then all he said was "What is your name?" I felt like we were starting over, as those were the first words he spoke to me when we met. I hope he sees it that way as well, as I find it unbearable to think of losing his friendship.

What will he do tomorrow? I don't contrive to give up the work, but if he betrays me I'll have no choice.

R. M. S.

JULY 8, 1836

Thomas says he will not tell, and that this is the funniest, most complicated prank he ever heard of. We were a bit awkward at first, but are now just as fast friends as we were.

R. M. S.

JULY 22, 1836

I thought I was strong and brown before! The work is hard, but there is a satisfaction in the steady chink of the hammer and the rhythms of the men laying ties. I would not want to do this forever, but for now I am feeding my family, and laying something by for winter; I have a steadfast, trustworthy friend, and I feel very powerful.

R. M. S.

These were the last words in Rose Marie's memoirs. I closed the book gently, and sat unseeing in the dusty attic. I thought about beginnings and endings, about roles and responsibilities, about railway ties and family ties, about history and romance. Making my way back downstairs to my school books, I picked up my pen, and began to write.

A Gourmet Dines
at the End of Track

⌒ by Constance Horne

With the noon meal cleared away, Bob moved around the kitchen refilling the water hopper and adding wood to the stove. He kept a wary eye on Big Hal. The last cook's helper had been hit with a flying fry pan in one of the cook's rages. That was the day that Bob, fifteen-years-old and just finished with the harvest, had walked into the railway camp at Moose Jaw Bone Creek looking for a job. Jeff, the foreman, had eyed him up and down, had said he was too skinny for manual labor and put him to work as cookee. He hated it.

The work gang was clearing and levelling the site for a supply depot so that in the spring of 1883 a track-laying crew could move in and push the rails further westward across the prairie. The idea of a railway spanning the country had caught the boy's imagination. His father's lonely farm seemed a dull place compared to helping to build the CPR. And now he was a cookee with Big Hal for a boss. Worse than farming. He wanted a real man's job.

He settled at the work table with a bucket of potatoes, a pan of water and a paring knife. Opposite him, Hal was trimming a roast of venison with the carving knife. All day, the cook had been nipping at his hidden bottle of home-made wine and was now muttering curses at the foreman who had ordered this extra work. Usually, the job was fairly easy. There were ten men in the crew and they ate and slept in a converted boxcar parked on the rails. One end was the dining room, then came the kitchen, the bunk house and, at the far end, an office and sleeping quarters for the foreman. The cook and his helper served three meals a day: oatmeal porridge, pancakes and syrup for breakfast; fried salt pork, mashed potatoes and carrots with pie for dinner; and for supper, baked beans and bread.

But yesterday the foreman had ordered a special meal to be served today after the gang had finished eating.

"The big boss is coming tomorrow to inspect the work," Jeff told the cook.

"Van Horne?" growled Hal.

Bob looked up eagerly. Even on an isolated prairie farm, he had heard of the famous General Manager of the Canadian Pacific Railway Company.

Jeff nodded. "He'll have his secretary with him, fellow by the name of Allenby. They'll stay for dinner. I want it to be something special."

Hal raised all sorts of objections, but Jeff was firm. In the morning he personally walked the two miles to an Indian encampment and bought deer meat and a cedar bark basket of dried saskatoon berries.

"Those are Van Horne's favourites — venison and saskatoon pie. Don't burn the meat to a crisp and see if you can make the pie crust a bit thinner than the usual slab."

He escaped before Hal could answer and Bob got the full blast of the cook's anger. So far it was only curses, but the boy nervously eyed the huge hands hacking at the meat.

Hal now looked up and focused on the young cookee.

"Spuds? Why are you peeling spuds again?"

"Jeff said he wanted them with the venison."

"Jeff said! Jeff said! I give the orders in this kitchen!"

Hal flung the carving knife. It passed inches from the Bob's ear and stuck in the door frame behind him.

Bob leapt up, overturning both the pail of potatoes and the pan of water. He raced through the dining room, down the metal steps and across the tracks to the woodpile, still lightly dusted by last night's frost. Crouched behind it, he heard Hal yell, "I quit!" in a roar that should have reached the gang at work beyond the bushes. But no one appeared. In a few minutes, Hal stomped down the steps, wearing his hat and coat and carrying his bed roll and duffel bag.

Shivering from cold and fear, Bob watched him tramp back along the track toward Regina.

As he cautiously straightened up, the foreman spoke from behind him.

"What the heck are you doing?"

Bob nodded toward the diminishing figure.

"Who's that?"

"Hal. He quit."

"What? He can't quit!" Jeff strode up to the track as if to follow the man, then stood looking helplessly after him. He groaned and rubbed his hand over his head, making his blond hair stick out in all directions. "What about Van Horne's dinner?" he growled. Then he gasped. "The venison! What did he do with the venison?" He raced up the steps into the boxcar.

Bob followed more slowly. Everything looked just as he had left it. The potatoes and peelings were still scattered across the floor but the water had soaked into the worn boards. The carving knife was still sticking in the door jamb. Bob pointed to it with a shaking finger. "He tried to kill me."

Jeff turned pale. "That maniac! If it wasn't for Van Horne, I'd say good riddance. Look, Bob, you'll have to cook the dinner for tonight."

"Me? No! I can't! I'm not a cook."

"I know, I know," the foreman said impatiently. "You hate working in the cook house. You want a man's job. You've told me that often enough. Listen, this dinner is real important to me. Van Horne is going to be pleased with the way the work is going. Now, if he gets a good dinner as well, I can ask him for a town job instead of always being stuck out at the end of track."

"But . . ." sputtered Bob. "I can't."

"Listen, here's a deal for you. If Van Horne likes the dinner, I'll give you a real job with a pick and shovel."

Bob stared at him for a moment. "You mean that?" Jeff nodded. The boy grinned briefly and then shook his head. "I can't do it alone."

"Fair enough. I'll get you a helper." There was still a lot of work to be done before the General Manager's inspection. Who could be spared? Who would be any use in the kitchen? Most of the men couldn't even speak English. "Ah, Wilf, the Limey. At least he'll be able to understand orders. I'll send him right in." At the door he turned back. "You're the boss of the cookhouse now, Bob."

Bob was still staring at the door when the little Englishman bounded in.

"So, where do you want me to start, Boss," asked Wilf.

"Huh?" Was this guy laughing at him? "You can clean up that mess," he said, pointing to the potatoes. "And then sweep the floor."

That felt good. The cook never did any sweeping.

"Right-ee-o," said Wilf cheerfully.

Now what? The meat was in the roasting pan, but when

was it supposed to go in the oven? Oh, gosh, the bread. Hal had left it in the oven. It might be burned. Quickly, he pulled out six loaf pans and sighed with satisfaction. The loaves were golden brown. He'd made a start. Well, not really. The bread was for the crew's supper at 5:30. How could he feed them and be ready for the Van Horne party at 6:30? And what about the special pies? Hal hadn't even started those.

Wilf was humming as he shuffled through a stack of enamel plates. "So what's the menu for the big cheese?" he asked over his shoulder.

"Roast venison, potatoes and carrots, and saskatoon pie," answered Bob.

"Rather skimpy meal for a gourmet," said Wilf.

"A what?"

"Gourmet. A man who appreciates his food. They say Van Horne is a real connoisseur of food and wine."

"He's out of luck then," said Bob morosely. "What are you doing anyway?"

"Finding unchipped plates for the guests. The setting should be worthy of the food. There we are: three whole plates, two good mugs and one chipped one. We'll give that to the boss. He's used to it."

He gave a mock salute as he waited for further orders.

"Uh, I don't suppose you could make a pie?" asked Bob without much hope.

Wilf squared his shoulders and lifted his chin. "Son,

before I was a failed farmer and a lowly navvy, I was pastry chef in the best hotel in Birmingham."

"You were a cook?"

"I was. Give me an apron and show me to the flour bin."

Soon the little man was rolling out pastry while Bob peeled potatoes. Wilf was humming again.

"Why did you quit cooking?" asked Bob. "You sure seem to like it."

"Oh, well, I got taken in by the propaganda. Come out to Manitoba, throw some wheat seed in the ground, watch it grow and then make a fortune selling it. No mention of the drought, the grasshoppers, the freezing winters in a tar-paper shack. I'd been working in a kitchen since I was four-teen and I thought I wanted a change. Well, I got it. From security to poverty in three years. Or, to put it another way, from cook to slave of the Canadian Pacific Railway."

"A man can get ahead in the CPR," said Bob. "I'd like to be a surveyor some day. I might make it, too, if I ever get a chance at a real job, not peeling spuds and carrots. Jeff promised me one, if Van Horne likes his dinner."

Wilf was stirring sugar and flour into the soaked berries to make the pie filling. He lifted up a spoonful and let it dribble back into the bowl. "We could make this a real gourmet meal," he said. "Soup, fish, meat, a sweet and a savory — that's the menu for a proper dinner."

"Fish? Where are we going to get fish out on the prairie?"

Wilf laughed. "Right you are. Well, we could substitute fowl for fish."

"And what the heck is a savory?" asked Bob.

"An ending to the meal. A spicy jelly, maybe. Or curried sweetbreads on toast."

"You're nuts!"

"Right again. Well, a good chef is adaptable. We'll serve coffee instead of the savory. I mean real coffee, not that muddy slop Hal makes."

He filled the pie shells and covered the berries with lattice crusts. As he turned from the oven, he said, "It just so happens that I have four prairie chickens in a sack under my bed. On Sundays, the German and I walk a mile or so down the track, make a fire and roast the birds."

"Huh! You'd only get a couple of mouthfuls out of one of them little things."

"Right, but it makes a change from the everlasting salt pork. Well, what do you say? Shall we go for it?"

Bob looked interested for a moment. Then he picked up another carrot and scraped it. "Naw. It would be too much work. Let's just feed the guys."

"It's up to you," said Wilf, "but the boss did say you get the new job if Van Horne likes the meal."

Bob stared at him. "You mean . . . ? The dirty rat! He knew I couldn't do it!"

"But you can. We can. We'll give the chief engineer a dinner that he'll rave about right across Canada. Then Jeff will have to keep his promise."

Bob frowned. Then grinned. Then nodded emphatically.

For the next few hours the "boss" of the kitchen plucked

chickens, cut up bread for stuffing, picked and chopped fresh wild sage, peeled more carrots and potatoes, boiled carrots and onions together then mashed them into a puree for soup, and found Wilf the ingredients and utensils he needed in an unfamiliar kitchen.

At one point, Wilf asked, "Do you know where Hal kept that wine he was always nipping at?"

"Oh no you don't!" said Bob.

"I don't want to drink it, you twit. It will flavour the gravy for the meat."

Luckily, there was enough left in the bottom of the jug.

At four o'clock they heard Van Horne's jigger arrive and went to the vestibule window to get a look at the great man. Jeff, freshly shaved and wearing a suit jacket over his flannel shirt, opened the door of the automobile body mounted on railway wheels. Two men stepped down. One was wearing a derby and an overcoat with a fur collar. He had a trim beard and piercing eyes. Bob shivered. It would take a very special meal to please him.

By six o'clock the gang had gulped down their beans and left. They reported that the chief engineer was in a good mood after inspecting the site.

"So it's up to us to keep him that way," said Wilf as he and Bob cleared off the table. "I don't suppose we have such a thing as a tablecloth?" Bob just looked at him. "No. Well, we do have hot water and a scrub brush. Clean oilcloth will have to do."

When Jeff had seated his guests, Bob came through the kitchen door carrying a battered tin tray with three bowls of soup and a plate of baking powder biscuits. He almost laughed aloud at the look on the foreman's face. Van Horne sat on one long side of the table with his secretary and Jeff opposite him. There was a stack of papers between them which the Manager kept referring to while he ate. Bob was afraid that he was paying no attention to the food. When he carried out the bowls, however, Van Horne called after him, "Good soup."

Wilf grinned and sent the boy out with the fowl. Compared to the way the workmen piled up their food, these plates looked skimpy. Each held a small roasted prairie chicken, a small mound of stuffing and a dab of saskatoon berry jelly.

The foreman scowled at Bob and muttered, "Where's the venison?"

Bob pretended he hadn't heard him.

After tasting the stuffing, Van Horne pushed the papers aside and concentrated on the chicken.

"Jeff, I know you don't allow liquor in camp," he said, "but a dinner like this just begs for a good wine. Mind if I bring in my own supply from the car?"

A chair scraped back. "I'll get it," said Allenby eagerly.

In a minute he returned with a square leather case containing three bottles and four crystal glasses. Van Horne filled the glasses with wine.

In the kitchen, Wilf punched Bob on the shoulder. "We've hooked him, me boy! Now for the entree."

He placed the venison in the center of a stoneware platter so that it hid the crack. He surrounded it with a ring of oven-roasted potatoes, whole boiled carrots and boiled onions and spooned the wine gravy over everything.

Jeff looked relieved when he saw the venison at last. He stood up to carve the roast that Bob placed before him.

Van Horne was now giving his full attention to the meal. "That looks delicious," he said.

"Smells great, too," Allenby agreed, as Jeff cut the first slice.

Both of them smiled at the server.

That job is mine! thought Bob.

He grinned when Van Horne asked, "Do you always eat like this, Jeff?"

"Heck, no! It's usually pork and spuds. I told the cook to do something special for you."

"Well, he sure did," said Van Horne. "Best meal I've ever eaten in a camp. Better than many a hotel for that matter." He laughed. "This is the first gourmet meal ever served in a CPR car in the Western Division."

As they cut up the pie, Bob and Wilf exchanged winks.

The General Manager heaved a sigh of contentment when Bob served the dessert. "Ah, saskatoon pie! My favourite."

"Somebody told me that," said Jeff with a grin.

With the tender crust melting in his mouth, Van Horne looked appraisingly at the foreman. "The way to a man's heart is through his stomach, eh? You must want something."

Jeff's cheeks reddened. "Yeah, that's right. Uh, I'd like a town job. See, I'm going to get married."

Van Horne nodded. "And the little woman wants a settled home." He paused while Bob poured his coffee. "Well, there are jobs opening up as we push westward. You've done good work here. And you've certainly inspired your cook. Call him out, will you, so we can thank him."

Jeff laughed and gestured at the boy. "It was Bob here. See, our cook quit this morning and I asked Bob to take over, not knowing he was a real chef. I'll make him chief cook, for sure."

Bob's arm went limp and the coffee pot dropped to the table with a bang.

"No, no," he sputtered. "You said . . . You promised . . . It wasn't me! It was Wilf. Wilf!" he yelped.

The little man appeared in the doorway, looking both proud and scared. Bob pointed at him accusingly. "He did it. He's the cook."

"What the devil's going on here?" asked Van Horne. He looked from the stuttering boy to the worried man in the apron to the red-faced foreman.

They all talked at once and eventually the whole story was told. Allenby tried to hide his smiles while it was going on, but at the end he let out a whoop. The Manager joined him in a long, hearty laugh.

"They say that laughter is good for the digestion," said

Van Horne, patting his stomach. "Jeff, you'll have to keep your promise to the boy. I liked the meal, so he gets the job he wants. As for you, Chef Wilf, you're too good to waste on a camp of navvies. When the CPR is running, there'll be a dining car on every passenger train. We'll need good cooks in the kitchens. Interested?"

"Right-ee-o," said Wilf. He beamed. "Boy oh boy! No more pick and shovel. A cook, now that's a real job."

Bob stared at him in wonder. How could anyone get excited about spending his whole life in a kitchen? He was the one who was getting the real job. He'd show them what a hard worker he was. He'd go places with the CPR he vowed to himself. He'd be a foreman like Jeff. And when the railway was finished? As he filled Van Horne's coffee mug the big man winked at him. Bob grinned widely. Maybe he'd even be Wilf's boss again someday.

Promises and Possibilities

∽ *by Barbara Haworth-Attard*

"Bubbling streams, peach orchards,
cheap land, grass for grazing. Make your Fortune!"

We huddled close together, the wide expanse of Saskatchewan prairie stretching before us.

"But where," Mother asked calmly, "are the bubbling streams the pamphlet promised. And there is no orchard."

Elsie and I exchanged a glance. When Mother spoke calmly, she was anything but calm.

"No orchards out here, Ma'am," Mr. Millward told her.

"Well, the pamphlet distinctly said *orchards*." Her voice was rising now. "It said *bubbling streams!*"

She meant the pamphlet that had brought our family all the way from our comfortable home in England to the Saskatchewan prairie. Once Dad had seen that pamphlet there was nothing for it, but that the whole family would move. The Boer War had recently ended and times were hard for many in England in 1903, but Dad was a clerk for a barrister. We had a roof over our heads, food for the table, coal for the fire and a maid to help Mother take care of us. *Us* were my sisters — Florence, sixteen, who spent all her time primping in her room, and Elsie, who was eleven and pretty much the best girl I knew; myself, twelve, going to the local grammar school as a day student; and my brother Edgar, who was eight and a real nuisance following me around everywhere. All in all things ran pretty well, every day flowing tidily into the next — until Dad got that pamphlet about Saskatchewan. He couldn't let it go.

"Land, Mary. A man has land and he has standing."

Mother had merely smiled, bending her head daintily over her embroidery, never dreaming he was serious. But now we stood watching prairie grass ripple, uncomfortably reminding my stomach of our time on the ship.

"Bubbling streams?" Mr. Millward repeated. Dad had hired Mr. Millward in Watson to drive us out and show us some of the cheap land where our fortune would be made.

"Well there's a slough over there," Mr. Millward said. He pointed to a spot in the grass that seemed greener than the rest and had a few thin trees sprouting from it.

"Orchards? There's willow and cottonwood. Did the pamphlet say anything about those? You'll want land with a slough on it," Mr. Millward continued.

"A slough?" Mother ventured when no one else dared ask.

"A waterhole," he answered.

Dad nodded his head wisely like he'd known about sloughs all his life. "Then I guess we'll take this quarter with the slough on it," he said.

Elsie, Edgar and I whooped with joy. We had our land. Mother appeared dazed. Florence's mouth gaped open, but it had been pretty slack since we'd boarded the train in Halifax. About the same time she'd stopped talking to anyone.

"Just what I would have picked," Mr. Millward said.

Dad's chest puffed out with pride. "I guess we're homesteaders then." He beamed at Mother, but she didn't seem to see, her eyes fixed on our land.

"So, what do you think, Dan?" Mr. Millward asked me.

"I think . . ." I swallowed and tried again. "I think . . ."

I saw Dad turn away slightly as he always did when I tried to speak. I was fine on the fringes of a group, unnoticed, but when singled out, speech fled. Mother told her friends I was painfully shy, while the doctor told Mother I had bad nerves. I felt a flush rise in my face and my legs begin to tremble as my eyes frantically searched the ground for the elusive speech. Elsie suddenly stuck her hand in mine. She knew how I felt despite the fact she could find words enough for both of us.

I knew what I wanted to say. The words were there now in my head, but when they reached my tongue, refused to leave. I wanted to tell Mr. Millward that the dome of blue sky above made me want to tuck myself into a small ball and shrink against the ground, yet at the same time I wanted to stretch out my arms and run through the waist-high waves of grass.

"It's big!" I finally spluttered. My voice came out too loud and spittle flew from my mouth.

Dad looked disgusted. I was completely crushed.

"It sure is big," Mr. Millward agreed. Strangely, he didn't seem to have noticed my affliction. The boys at school certainly had, and the masters too. The last time I'd been called upon to answer a question, I'd stood at the front of the class, blushing and shaking. Finally the teacher had told me to sit down as there was not enough time in all eternity to wait for me to speak — and write out my answer one hundred times. My classmates hadn't let me forget that one.

We unloaded the two wagons. Mr. Millward tossed a small plow to the ground. "You'll need this to build your home," he told me.

Elsie and I exchanged another glance and she shrugged. We had no idea what he meant.

Then Mr. Millward turned to Dad. "You'll want to get right back and file your land," he said. "It's late in the year, so you'll need supplies for the winter."

He bent down and picked up a hard, dried brown chip from the dust and handed it to Edgar. "Give that to your mother and find some more," he told us.

Edgar turned the chip over and over in his hand. "What is it?"

"Your fuel."

"But what is it?" Mother asked.

"Buffalo dung."

Mother's eyes widened. "Edgar, you put that filthy thing down right now."

Edgar dropped it like a hot coal.

"Do you see any wood around here, missus?" Mr. Millward asked.

"No."

"Well, that . . ." Mr. Millward kicked the brown chip with his foot ". . . is what is going to keep you warm when February blizzards and cold like you've never known before, hits you."

He and Dad turned the wagon on its side and stretched a large piece of white canvas over it.

"This will keep you fine until you get your place built," Mr. Millward said.

"That's our house? We're all to stay in there — together?" Florence shrieked. First thing she had said in days.

Mr. Millward shrugged. "You could sleep out under the stars, but I expect the mosquitoes will soon drive you in. That's another thing. Get a fire going before nightfall. It'll help keep the biting bugs away. And keep that shelter flap closed or you'll not sleep tonight."

He turned to the plow. "Now, boy," he said to me, "what do you know about plowing?"

"Nothing, sir." His question took me so by surprise, I found myself answering without hesitation.

"Well, you're going to have to learn fast because plowing is going to build your house. Watch closely." He harnessed up the horse to the plow and dug a deep furrow into the land. "You try now."

Easy, I thought, as I took the reins and wrapped them around my hands like he had. But the horse wouldn't behave for me, dragging me along while the plow bounced and scraped across the soil.

"Keep at it," Mr. Millward said. "You'll get the knack soon. While your father's gone you dig a fireguard. Fifteen or twenty furrows."

He spoke with such assurance that I could plow, that I found myself beginning to believe I could actually work the blade into the dirt as he had.

"Keep it the same thickness, then pull up the sod and cut it into one-by-two-foot rectangles with your spade and pile it carefully. Those are going to be your walls."

"What?" Mother exclaimed. Her voice was an octave higher than normal.

"There's no wood on the prairies so you build your house out of the land," Mr. Millward told her. "A sodhouse."

"I will not live in a dirt house like a — a barbarian!" Mother glared at Dad.

Dad couldn't think of a thing to say. He looked at the sky and land, anywhere but at Mother.

After a moment, Mr. Millward cleared his throat. "Sod-houses are mighty warm in the winter and plenty cool in summer. When your husband and I get to town I'll have some folks come out and lend you a hand to set up. It's just your first house, Missus, then later you can build a wooden one. Everyone starts out that way. Anyway . . ." he added hastily after a quick glance at Mother's stony face ". . . we have to go. Good luck to you all."

"I'll be back day after tomorrow, Mary," Dad said. "I expect it'll take me that long to tie up all the loose ends." He quickly climbed on the wagon. "Now Daniel, you help your mother." But he said it as if it was something he was supposed to say, and I felt myself shrivel inside. I knew Dad didn't think me much good for anything and I suspected he might be right.

We watched Dad and Mr. Millward until they were tiny spots on the horizon, and then vanished altogether. We were alone. Alone in a strange land.

"I'm going to lie down," Mother said. "First that awful ship . . . I'll never get the stench out of my clothes, then sitting on that train for days. Now this." She swept a hand in front of her, while tears ran down her face. "It's too much to bear." She opened the flap of canvas and went into the shelter. Florence began to wail and followed her.

Elsie, Edgar and I huddled together, until I noticed Elsie shivering. I went in and got a blanket to wrap around the three of us.

"I'm hungry," Edgar announced.

I found a loaf of bread and broke off a chunk and handed

it to him. We sat and chewed, listening to Mother and Florence cry. I was mad at them, but at the same time knew that Mother and Florence were more familiar with embroidery and parties and polite conversation than cooking, dung fires and sod houses. I shook my head slowly. We'd never make it here in this country and, for some reason, that made me sad.

Mother came out once, hair tangled around her face, buttons on her blouse askew. She looked around vaguely. "I need the facilities." She turned in a circle, unable to decide what to do.

"Maybe over there?" I pointed to a lone tree near the slough.

She headed in that direction, and a moment later returned to the shelter.

Before bed I took the horse down to the slough and let it drink. I'd left the plow harnessed to her because I was afraid I wouldn't be able to get it back on again once off. Why I worried about that I don't know. I had no plans to plow, but she didn't seem to mind dragging it along behind.

I stood at the slough's edge as evening washed down in pink and purple, and the vastness and quiet of the prairie enveloped me. I leaned against the horse's flank, taking comfort in its warmth and the fact it required nothing of me except food and water. As before, I felt torn. I wanted to be like Florence and whimper, yet I found myself enjoying the peace. There was no one I had to talk to. No one to single me out and question me. I almost felt normal.

The next morning Mother and Florence refused to come out of the shelter, except for a brief trip to the facilities. Elsie and I wandered around with Edgar. We were scared to go far, the land still being too large. I'd softened up some old buns in water for their breakfast, and we shared the last precious orange Dad had bought us on the train. I sucked on that skin all morning, enjoying the change from mealy bread in my mouth.

"Do you think we'll go home?" Elsie asked.

"I don't know," I told her. I never had bad nerves or painful shyness around Elsie. In fact, she'd probably heard me talk more than anyone. "Do you want to go?"

"Do you?" she asked me back.

At first I had no words in either my brain or mouth to answer that, but then I did. "No!"

I looked at her pinched face, and Edgar's tear-stained cheeks and knew I had to do something. This was all we had, this piece of land. I didn't want to go back to England because everyone there either made fun of me or felt sorry for me. I was starting to get used to the space all around me here. There were promises and possibilities here.

"No. I don't want to go back. Edgar gather up some of those buffalo chips," I ordered. "Elsie get out the tea things." I soon had a fire going and water from the slough boiling in the kettle.

Elsie spread a white table cloth over the prairie dirt. She

carefully unwrapped the china cups and saucers and set them out with Mother's silver tea pot and strainer. I measured in the tea, poured boiling water over top, then opened a box of biscuits Mother had brought with us for a special occasion. I gave one to Edgar who settled down happily to munch on it.

"Mother, Florence," I called. "Tea's ready."

Mother came out, saw us sitting on the ground, the tea set before us and her face began to crumple.

"As soon as we're done here . . ." I told her, pretending I didn't see. I was having no trouble with words now; they were pouring from me ". . . I'm going to make a start plowing those furrows and get the sod ready for the house. Elsie and Edgar can help stacking."

Mother's face twisted further, then slowly straightened out to look the way I remembered from back home. She patted her hair, pulled out a couple pins, then shoved them back in. "Florence," she called, her voice shaky, but firm. "Florence. Come and have your tea, then help Dan. Edgar . . ." Her voice broke, then gathered strength. "Get me some more of those . . . chips. We'll need a good hot dinner after working all day."

Songs for the Dead

∽ by Cathy Beveridge

There was, thought Jonathon, something peculiar about the silence of this coal miner's funeral. It was a silence stretched tight between grief and relief — grief for the dead man's widow and his son, Ian; relief for his own family, standing now on the other side of the grave. It was a silence that stretched across the cemetery, silencing the minister's attempts at consolation, the widow's muffled sobs and, finally, the small yellow goldfinch perched on Jonathon's shoulder.

The minister nodded and four men, including Jonathon's father, stepped forward. Slowly they lowered the pine box into the open grave. Jonathon's eyes lingered on Ian's. For almost a year the boy had occupied the desk beside him at school. Tomorrow it would be empty.

Thud! A shovelful of dirt landed on the coffin. Jonathon watched the hands that gripped the shovels. Clean hands, he noted, recalling his father's attempts to scrub the coal dust from the creases of his palms and scrape the black grit from beneath his fingernails.

Ian's hands would be the same soon. The Company had already assured Ian's mother that there would be a job sorting coal at the tipple for him, the eldest boy. And in just a few years, Ian would be working underground where the real money could be made.

Underground! His father worked underground. Jonathon had been into the mine once with his father, into the cold tunnels, as black as a raven's wing. Ian's father had died in that darkness, in the guts of the mine. And yet, he had not died in darkness. His life had been extinguished in a burst of light — a sudden explosion of gas.

Methane gas! It seeped from the coalface and lay waiting in pockets — unseen, unsmelt, unheard, untouched and untasted — awaiting a spark from a pick or the flame of a lamp. Then, the explosion ripped through the tunnels, up the slopes and burst from the mine entrance. Then, the explosion extinguished a man's life. Then, the explosion forced young teenage boys like himself to leave school and work in the black guts of the mountain.

Jonathon waited until the long line of men and women clad in black had started back towards town. "Hey, look, it's J-J-Jon-a-th-th-th-on," said a boy's voice behind him.

"With his w-w-w-wild c-c-c-an-ar-ar-ar-y," added another.

Jonathon fought the impulse to correct them. Couldn't they see the distinct black cap and wing feathers that distinguished his American goldfinch? The little yellow and black bird twittered and sang.

"G-g-g-oing to sch-sch-school tomorrow?" mocked one of the boys. "Or, or, or are you going off into the w-w-wilderness?"

Jonathon stared at a bluejay in a neighbouring tree. It had been almost a year since his family had arrived in the Crowsnest Pass and he had started school. Most days he endured the humiliation of having to stammer an answer in front of the class. But on the days that he could not endure the mockery of his classmates, he escaped into the surrounding hills. It was on one such day late in the summer that he had found the little goldfinch, her wing torn from her body. Knowing that she would never fly again, he had picked her up intending to wring her delicate neck. But then she had opened her beak in song and Jonathon had taken her home instead. Now she perched on his shoulder, his constant companion.

"You boys there, get along," called a woman's voice.

"Got to g-g-g-go!" hissed one of the boys, striding towards town.

Jonathon smiled at the woman. "Th-th-th-thanks," he called. He spoke so seldom that his voice seemed cracked and jagged. Jonathon's goldfinch sang in his ear. Songs for the dead. Songs for Ian's father.

Leaving the cemetery, Jonathon mulled over a thought that had preoccupied him for the past few days. From atop the hill, he surveyed the huge boulders left several years earlier by the great rockslide of 1903. Then he followed a familiar trail into the hills towards a large shaft that had been dug into the earth — a ventilation shaft to keep fresh air circulating inside the mine. Nearby, Jonathon brushed the leaves from the three makeshift wooden crosses that marked the shallow graves. He had found the swallows lying lifeless near the timbers of the shaft just hours before the explosion in the tunnel below. Then, he had wondered why they had died. Now, he knew, or at least he thought he knew.

Jonathon moved noiselessly through the dusk toward their small wooden house. He could see the silhouettes of his father, his father's partner in the mine, Joe, and another man that he could not distinguish.

"The Company says the ventilation system's good and well-maintained too," said Joe.

Another voice that Jonathon recognized as Mario Antonelli's murmured skeptically.

Jonathon made a wide circle past the three men. "You're late," his father growled. "Ma wants that kindling cut." Jonathon pulled the axe free from the chopping block. Whistling, his goldfinch hopped onto the woodpile.

"I heard there were problems with the generators this week — kept shutting down," said Mario. "Heard there's too much methane in this mine. Pockets everywhere. You both ought to think about switching to those new safety lamps."

Joe shook his head. "Light's too poor. Besides the Company says we don't need them here."

"The Company doesn't want to bear the cost of replacing the old lamps, that's all," replied Mario. "One man's dead already. Maybe if he hadn't had an open flame . . ." His voice trailed off.

Jonathon kept the time of their silence with the rhythm of the axe.

Finally, his father spoke. "Perhaps, but you can't mine what you can't see. It's tough enough mining with an open flame and I can't afford to take less coal out of the mine. That'd mean a cut in wages."

Joe leaned over the railing. "You going to the meeting tomorrow to hear the results of the inquiry?"

"I'll be there. We'll all be there, I expect," said Jonathon's father.

"And it'll be the same thing we always hear after a man dies or gets hurt and there's a safety inquiry," said Mario. "They'll tell us that the mine's safe, that we don't need the new lamps. But the fact is that there's a whole lot better chance of knowing if there's methane gas around with those safety lamps than with the open-flame ones, never mind the fact that they ain't so likely to ignite it."

After the men had left, Jonathon's father joined him at the woodpile. "I-I-I found three dead birds," managed Jonathon, his face red with his efforts. "B-b-b-b." He gave up. "In-in the ventilation shaft."

"You aren't skipping out of school again, are you?"

Jonathon ignored his question "B-be-before the blast." His bottom lip quivered but he pressed on. "N-n-no blood or broken bones."

His father studied Jonathon. "And you think that it was gas that killed those birds?" Jonathon nodded. His father frowned, extended a hand to the chanting goldfinch and held the bird on his fingers.

"Y-y-yes!" exclaimed Jonathon.

His father smiled. "Anything might have killed those birds, son — bad water, bad food, fright." He returned the bird to Jonathon's shoulder and climbed the porch steps.

"Y-y-y-you must use the safety lamps!" The words exploded from Jonathon. The goldfinch gave a shrill trill.

Jonathon's father's eyes narrowed. "Silent be that bird before the son advises the father," he said curtly before entering the house.

Jonathon embedded the axe in the chopping block and gathered the kindling. He should have known that he would not be able to change his father's mind. His father had never listened to him before. But this time a strange fear gripped him — this time his father was wrong.

There was trouble with the generator again the next day.

Jonathon could hear the big fans start and stop as he maneuvered across the hillside. His goldfinch chirped steadily, then fell silent. Jonathon peered into a ventilation shaft. A sparrow lay on a ledge not far below, its tiny feet extended upwards. Jonathon bent to touch its still-warm body. His goldfinch cheeped softly. Three other sparrows lay belly up nearby. From the dark hole of the mine came the clinking of picks and the scraping of shovels. Quickly, Jonathon swept the birds together and piled rocks over all but one, tucking its body into his jacket pocket. Then he ran to find his father.

The safety inquiry meeting had already begun and the hall was filled. Jonathon ducked inside. His father was near the front, along one side of the room, but there was no way to reach him. Jonathon pressed the sparrow's body against his.

"The inspectors have assured us that the mine is safe," said a Company man. "The ventilation system in this mine is one of the finest around and methane levels were found to be low."

The man in front of Jonathon raised his hand and, once acknowledged, rose to speak. "Are we going to get the new lamps?"

"The Company does not intend to make the safety lamps mandatory. While these lamps do aid in the detection of methane gas, their reduced light causes other hazards for the miners. That will be left to the discretion of each of you."

Jonathon studied the crowd. He had to tell them about the dead birds. Never before had he spoken in front of so many people. Slowly, he raised his arm.

"Yes, the young lad at the back." All eyes turned towards Jonathon. He opened his mouth, felt the beads of sweat trickle down his forehead.

"Did you want to say something, lad?"

In the front corner of the room, Jonathon's father had risen to his feet. He stood scowling, his arms crossed in front of his chest. Jonathon stared at the rows of eyes. Then suddenly he turned and bolted from the hall.

Laughter chased him past the mine, to the river and beyond. He crashed through the brush towards a grassy clearing and into an old trapper's cabin he had found months ago. Curling up in one corner, he removed the dead sparrow from his pocket, cradled his goldfinch in his arms and slept.

The night was warm but his dreams were cold. Dead chickadees and robins fell from the sky like raindrops. Hawks and owls collapsed mid-flight and collided with the earth. Jonathon woke drenched in sweat. Beside him, his little goldfinch twittered, pecked at his hair and ruffled her feathers. Beside her lay the body of the dead sparrow he had found yesterday.

The first rays of sun crept over the slide and awakened the birds. Waxwings called and chickadees replied. Jonathon rose to his feet, placed his goldfinch on his shoulder and collected the dead sparrow. With the mist still lying in the valley, he padded through the brush. Dawn lay across the mine entrance. The morning shift had not yet arrived. He climbed to the timbers above the entrance to wait. His goldfinch sang softly.

The miners' voices reached him first. Soon they would assemble here, some holding the new safety lamps they had bought themselves; others, like his father, with their Company-issued open-flame lamps. Then they would begin the long walk into the mine, into the gas that had killed the birds.

Jonathon caught sight of his father. The boy stood upright on the timber above the entrance and held up the dead sparrow. "L-l-look!" he cried before he could think about what he was doing. The men looked up. Jonathon dropped the sparrow at his father's feet. "Th-th-the g-g-gas that killed this bird will kill you."

The men murmured. "Take the boy home," said one man kindly to Jonathon's father. "He's not quite right, poor lad."

Jonathon's father shifted uncomfortably. "The boy found dead birds near the shaft where the explosion occurred," he said quietly.

"Problems with the ventilation system," called one voice.

"It's unsafe, it is. They ought to make safety lamps mandatory."

"Nonsense! This mine's as safe as any."

"Move along. I've got me a family to feed."

A chorus erupted from the men and the crowd started to push past Jonathon's father.

"Y-y-y-you can't go in there, father!" Jonathon's voice burst from him.

His father sighed. "I have to, Jonathon."

"N-n-no!" Jonathon's goldfinch sang out with the rising sun and the men fell silent listening to her sweet melody. Jonathon collected the little, yellow bird in his hands. "T-t-take her," he said softly. "T-t-t-take her with you into the mine. If she st-st-stops singing, come out." His eyes pleaded with his father.

Joe motioned for Jonathon's father to join the line of men.

Jonathon's father hesitated.

"P-p-please!" pleaded Jonathon.

"Go ahead," said one of the other miners. "What harm can it do? Besides it might calm the boy some."

Jonathon's father smiled. "All right, son. I'll take your bird to work today. A bit of music might be nice underground." A few men laughed and passed under Jonathon, their lunchboxes banging, their lamps swinging.

"You're a darn fool," said Joe to Jonathon's father as he brushed past him and disappeared into the darkness.

Jonathon scrambled down. Gently, he lifted his goldfinch from his own shoulder and placed it on his father's. She cheeped and chorused.

"Go on home, Jonathon," his father said gently. "Your

mother's worried about you." He smiled before following the others underground.

The teacher's voice drifted through the classroom. Jonathon stared out the window, Ian's empty desk beside him.

A long, shrill blast filled the air. The mine whistle! The class fell silent. One long whistle meant trouble. Jonathon sprinted from the school, raced down the boardwalks and tore through the dirt roads that led to the mine. He reached the mine entrance before most of the townspeople and positioned himself close to the timbers that framed the tunnel.

Questions swirled through the assembling crowd — questions that nobody could answer. Finally, several men supporting each other, dragged themselves out into the fresh air. Jonathon searched for his father. "Explosion, in seam four." The words circled his head. "Entire room collapsed." The crowd opened up to make way for them. "Flash of light. Boom."

Another group of men stumbled into the sunshine. Women searched for their husbands through their tears. "Big blast. No telling how many." Children clutched their mother's skirts. Jonathon dug his fingers into the rough wood and waited.

A Canada goose called overhead. Jonathon looked upwards.

"Jonathon." His father's voice. His father stood half in darkness, half in the sunlight, one arm hanging uselessly in front of him.

Jonathon ran to him, encircling him with his arms, lifting him against his own body. His father leaned wearily against him. "You were right, Jonathon." Wincing with pain, he unfolded the hand that hung in front of his chest. Cradled in his fingers was the dead body of Jonathon's goldfinch. "I'm sorry, son."

"Sh-sh-she, she, stopped singing?" asked Jonathon softly.

"I'd set her down on my lunchbox not far from me. She sang all morning and then, just before lunch, I noticed that she'd stopped. I told Joe that we ought to get out." His eyes fought back the tears. "But he wouldn't go." He looked back at the mine entrance. "I couldn't convince him, so I started out on my own. About halfway, I felt the blast. There was no point trying to go back in." Silent tears fell on Jonathon's shoulders. "Maybe if we'd had one of those safety lamps, like you said . . ."

Jonathon took the tiny yellow bird from his father's hand. He smiled at the sky, bright with sunlight. Somewhere above him, a goldfinch sang.

The Ballot

⌁ by Catherine Goodwin

The October morning was sunny with a cool breeze that hinted of winter. I dressed carefully, choosing my new button boots and green ankle length suit, a large gold broach pinned to the jacket. Then, squaring my shoulders, I hurried downstairs, the soles of my button boots tapping out the rhythm of my heartbeat. Today I would vote.

My father, Alistair McLennan, was already at breakfast. He, too, had been up early. He stood as I entered the room, extending his hand to pull back a chair for me.

"Good morning," I said. Father glanced at my clothes.

"Where are you going, Elizabeth?" he asked.

"I'm going to the school, Father," I answered. "To Lord Roberts, where the polling — "

"You are not thinking to vote, surely!"

His words circled around me, plummeting over and over into my ear. Not vote, not thinking to vote, surely, surely! I rearranged the linen napkin in my lap. I said nothing. What a coward I am!

"Elizabeth, you know my beliefs," he persisted, a few decibels too loud for the small dining room.

I clenched my hands, digging my nails into the flesh of my palms and fought back tears. A hot blush spread from my cheekbones to my chin. It was not the first time Father's outbursts had frightened me. My tongue was dry and I felt like a young child again. I did, indeed, know Alistair Mc-Lennan's beliefs. Had heard them all my life! A woman's place is in the home, he believed, not at the ballot box. He was against the vote. Plain and simple. And Mother had not disagreed. But, in truth, there was never a need. For women were still struggling to *achieve* the right while Mother was alive.

Surely that was behind us. Now women held the franchise. It had been over two years since Sir William shocked the province, extending the ballot to include both sexes. It was a step that had taken the women of Ontario nearly thirty years to achieve. I reached for my water glass and swallowed with difficulty. The inclusion of women in the franchise act should be enough, but apparently it was not. What had become law in 1917 remained unacceptable to my father. I knew his opinions. And yet, somehow, I had hoped . . .

"Elizabeth, you are a McLennan. The women of the Mc-Lennan family do not vote."

"But, Father," I pleaded, "I thought, I hoped, Sir William himself . . ." Words tumbled out of my mouth in spurts, the end of one attached to the beginning of the next. I tried again to explain, "Father, I am permitted to vote. Don't you see? The premier himself has extended the franchise."

"Sir William Hearst is a fool!" Father pushed away from the table, his chair scraping against the hardwood floor as he stood. From the hallway he turned and pointed at me.

"What's more, the women would never have won the franchise had the men of the Dominion not been overseas, fighting the war. But I'll tell you one thing, Elizabeth Mc-Lennan, I will not be made a fool, along with Sir William. Do you hear? You will not vote and that's final! Not today, not any day, for as long as you hold the name of McLennan. Is that clear?"

I lowered my head, speechless, and remained that way until I heard Father's footsteps fade into the braided rug upstairs. The grandfather clock chimed behind me, its deep tone resonating off the high ceiling in the hallway. Seven o'clock! The polls were officially opened. I sat upright, my spine against the leather of my chair. Hot tears stung my eyes. For weeks, I had carefully clipped and trimmed every bit of news I could find in the *Free Press*. It was October 20, 1919. I was twenty-four years old and had never voted before. No woman in Ontario had. This was the very first ballot for us. A few days ago, the newspaper had predicted record turnouts at the polls. In our city, 31,695 Londoners were entitled to vote and I had believed I would be one of them.

"Shall we walk together to the polls?" Edna Holmes asked, speaking as I opened the heavy oak door. We lived in a yellow brick house in a quiet neighbourhood north of the shops and businesses. Edna was our neighbour. The twin houses shared one wall and the front porch, but each home had a separate entrance and walkway.

Edna studied my face. "Whatever is wrong?" she asked.

My eyes darted toward the stairs. Where was Father? Could he hear? I stepped over the wooden stoop, pulling the door half-closed behind me. "You had best go ahead without me, Mrs. Holmes," I whispered.

She glanced at the new clothes I was wearing and then back toward the front door. "You are coming to vote, are you not?"

Weeks ago, Edna and I had ridden the street car to the edge of the city where the Thames River forks. Dundas Street had taken on its usual hum. Along the busier sections, the new hydro electric signs hung outside shops. Motor cars clogged the street, their engines frightening the horses as farm wagons, laden with the fall harvest, headed toward the market at the centre of town. A crowd had already gathered outside the courthouse, all of us eager to add our names to the eligible voters list. Three times since that trip, I had scanned the completed list which was posted on walls and poles throughout the city. My name was there. I could vote.

"You are going to vote, Elizabeth," Edna repeated firmly.

"Shh, lower your voice, Mrs. Holmes," I pleaded.

Edna Holmes was a good deal older than I and had waited a lifetime for the right to vote. She had twice been a delegate to Toronto to petition Sir William. A sickening sensation churned in the pit of my stomach. What could I tell her? Edna Holmes spoke her mind. No one would ever forbid *her* to vote. But, then, she had never been a McLennan!

"It's one thing to win the right to a ballot, Elizabeth," she said now. "But quite another to use it."

"You don't understand, Mrs. Holmes. What choice do I have? Father has made up his mind. I don't know what I could possibly say to change things."

"Whatever has happened, Elizabeth, there are two things you must do now," Edna continued. "First, you must decide what it is you *want* to say — "

"And the second?" I interrupted, anxious to end the conversation before Father came downstairs.

"You must *say* it!" Edna responded before going alone to vote.

A short time later, Father also left for the polling station. I watched from the upstairs window until his hat could no longer be seen beneath the canopy of maple trees. I am such a coward. Decide what it is you want to say and then say it, Edna had advised. Instead, I said nothing at all.

The stack of newspaper clippings lay on the corner of my writing table. I scrunched them into a tight ball. "Oh, whatever is the use of having a vote if I am unable to use it," I cried, tossing the heap into my waste basket.

For nearly an hour I paced before the window. A wide band of sunlight filtered through the lace curtains and danced, particle by particle, across the quilt at the foot of my bed. I was miserable. I knew how Father felt, but I had not mentioned that I intended to vote until the very day of the election. Why hadn't I? Now I had only until six o'clock when the polls closed to change his mind.

Over and over I thought of what I would say. I would tell Father why the vote was important to me. Things had changed while Father was overseas serving with the troops. The whole Empire was at war, but here, in our home on Princess Avenue, we had found peace. The change was gradual, but began almost as soon as the soldiers left London. Mother was not well then. I took a job at McCormick's factory, packaging biscuits during the days. Most evenings I spent with Mother and Edna Holmes.

Edna spoke often of the suffrage movement in Ontario. How women had initially banded together under the guise of literary clubs and discussed the need of a ballot. The more I discovered about the early suffragists, the more I began to see things differently.

One afternoon, Edna invited me to her women's meeting and Mother agreed I could go.

Most of the women were a lot older than I, closer to Edna's age than my own. I chose a chair near the door and sat down, for I was shy and had no intention of becoming involved in the proceedings. I smelled wood burning in a stove by the parlour door and polish on the furniture around me. The room was warm and noisy with ideas, the voices melting and blending together.

I knew nothing of the women before me, nothing of their families or lives. I knew little about the Council of Women, only that it was a national organization whose mandate was to improve the quality of life for all. But here was a group of proud Canadian women. I gazed around the parlour from face to face. These women wanted the right to vote. One emotion shone on those faces as they spoke of that right. And that one emotion was determination.

I thought about that determination as I waited downstairs for Father to return. I was resolved to vote and, this time, I would say so. But as Father turned his key in the lock, a small empty feeling started to gnaw inside me again. Just speak, I told myself. Just say it!

"Father," I began before I lost my nerve. "I would like to tell you something."

"Yes, what is it?"

I opened my mouth but could scarcely force out the words. "I shall vote today," I stammered.

Father drew a deep breath and let it out slowly. He held his gloves in one hand, removing his hat with the other. "I forbid you to speak of the vote, Elizabeth. My mind is made up and it will not be changed," he said.

What choice did I have? I gave up.

All day, in fifteen-minute intervals, the Westminster chimes on our clock reminded me that the polling station would soon close. I grew desperate. Father sat in the parlour reading. I could not see him directly, only the corner of his book and the legs of his trousers stretched out on the rug. Toward dinner time, I peered around the corner and saw nothing at all.

"Father?" I called. No reply. I went to the foot of the stairs and called again. Still nothing. I saw him then through the brocade drapes at the back of the house. He was in the garden by the boxwood hedge, clippers in hand, his back to our house. I watched as he carefully trimmed the leaves, cutting each twig that had outgrown the others. Father likes order, I said aloud. And hearing my own voice, I was struck by a thought.

It was true that the McLennan women did not vote, but it was the *men* in the family who had made that choice. I grabbed my hat and stretched my fingers into cotton gloves, shutting the front door quietly behind me. I was the first woman in the McLennan family with the *right* to vote. The first to begin a new tradition and there was no time to lose.

Lord Roberts School, a short distance away, had been built three years earlier. The building was bright and warm. Some boasted it was the most modern school in the city and the pride of the neighbourhood. I couldn't imagine a more fitting spot for the election.

Although late in the day, carriages and motor cars were still pulling to the curb. I hurried to the boys' entrance of the school and took my place in the line at the door. Men and women greeted each other, their words swallowed up by the din of the crowd. A celebration, that's what it was. And I was a part of it.

"Elizabeth McLennan," I said clearly, enunciating each of the seven syllables of my name for the outside scrutineer. A large Union Jack flew at the entrance and another hung inside beside the portrait of the king. My eyes scanned the trappings of a polling station. Two polling clerks. The screened polling booth and before me a metal box, the words, Dominion of Canada, stencilled boldly across the front.

I am a daughter of the Empire, a citizen of the Dominion and the first McLennan woman to vote, I reminded myself as I moved down the line, closer and closer to the polling clerks. It wouldn't take long. I knew exactly how to vote on both the referendum and the ballot that would determine London's next representative to Ontario's fifteenth Legislature. I imagined myself behind the screened booth, feeling the pencil between my fingers. A large black "X" four times on my referendum ballot. No! I did not want the Temperance Act repealed. It prohibited the sale of liquor and it made sense to me. No! I did not want beer sold through government agencies. No! I did not want the act amended to permit the sale of beer in hotels. No! I was not in favour of other spirits and malts being sold through government agencies.

Then I thought of the second ballot. My heart pumped rapidly. This is how it feels to vote, I thought. Soon I would choose between Sir Adam Beck and Dr. H. A. Stevensen, our electoral candidates.

I was third in line to the ballot when I felt the strong grip above my elbow. And there, not an inch from my face, was Father.

"How dare you!"

"Father," I began. "Please, Father, I have never disobeyed you before, but I am begging you now. Please, let me have my vote."

"Get to the car, Elizabeth!"

"Let her vote!" said a women behind me. "The right is hers!"

Several men murmured in agreement. "Give her the vote, man!"

"Get to the car," Father repeated slowly.

My eyes darted from one woman to another. In those faces, the faces of strangers, I saw something of myself. In every village and town across Ontario, women were voting and I was one of them. It had taken generations, but we had finally taken our place and I was not prepared to give mine up.

"No, Father, I will not get in the car," I said quietly. "I respect your right to an idea, but I am entitled to a vote."

"I am going to the car, Elizabeth, and if you wish to remain a McLennan, you will follow me," Father said, removing his hand from my arm. "Have you no pride in who you are?"

"I do, Father," I answered quietly. "I have great pride. The McLennans are women, as well as men, and I am the first with the right of a ballot."

Father stared as though seeing me for the first time. The line moved forward then and a man behind us took a step closer.

"I'm a Prohibitionist," he said to Father. "And deadly against the repeal of the Temperance Act. There's an important decision to be made today, a decision that will affect all of us and, by George, we need the women's vote!"

Father didn't answer. He, too, was against the sale of alcohol. His gaze went from the women standing shoulder-to-shoulder beside the men then back to me. An expression I had rarely seen flickered across his face, a slight wrinkling of his brow, a softening in his blue eyes. Then a deep red glow crept upward from under the stiff collar of his shirt.

"I am going to the car, Elizabeth," he said finally.

"Father, wait," I called, watching his back as he took the stairs, but not once did he turn.

I walked from Lord Roberts, my head high and had just reached the pavement when I spotted the Ford Runabout, parked across the street, a short distance away. Father stood at the curb. He opened the passenger door as I crossed the street. He had waited, waited to take me home. I was still a part of the McLennan family. And, as of today, McLennan women voted along with their men. When the polls closed in London, my ballot would be tallied. Along with the other citizens of Ontario, I would decide the fate of the Temperance Act and choose who would represent me in government. I had known for some time what it was I wanted to say. Today, I had found the courage to say it.

To Begin Again

⌐— by Carolyn Pogue

A man in a suit and bowler hat walked quickly across the platform. His footsteps echoed in the lonely train station. "You the Home Child?" he asked. "The kid from England?"

"Yessir," I said.

"You're the one." He signalled a red-cap to carry my trunk and walked away fast. I followed him off the platform, out of the station to a row of waiting cabs. Soon the horses were trotting up Yonge Street. Toronto was crowded with horses and buggies, electric street cars, gentlemen on bicycles and ladies strolling on the sidewalk. Outside the cab, life looked exciting. Inside the cab, life was silent. The master didn't tell me his name or say a word, just kept looking at me out of the corner of his eye. My stomach felt tight.

We stopped in front of a tall brick house. No one came out to meet us.

I followed the master into the dimly lit hall. He left me as a tall woman wearing a brown rustling dress walked slowly down the wide oak staircase, peering at me over her spectacles. "So you're the new one, eh? What do they call you?"

"I beg your pardon, madam?"

"What's your *name*, girl?"

"Gwen Peters, madam," I said.

"You're rather thin, Gwen Peters. I was hoping for one a little stronger than the last one. The English send the scrawny ones to Canada, I guess." She snorted a little laugh. "Have you been in service before?"

"No, madam." In reply, she clucked her tongue.

A tall thin woman about a hundred years old came down the hall. "This one says her name is Gwen Peters," the woman told her.

To me she added, "Mrs. Richards is the cook and you're to mind her *absolutely*. You'll learn your duties from her." She glared at me once more, then went into the sitting room and closed the door.

"Don't stand there gawking," said Mrs. Richards. "Your room is on the third floor, white door at the end. Take the back stairs, hang up your hat, and be down in the kitchen in five minutes."

The white door creaked when I opened it. The little room had a sloped ceiling and one small round window. It contained one rickety bed with a holey cover, a small table and a washstand holding a chipped basin and pitcher. The room was hot and stuffy. I stood on the bed and tried to open the window, but it was painted shut.

I sat on the edge of the bed and took a deep breath. "This is the beginning of my Canadian adventure," I said out loud. "Someday I will make up a play about this adventure, and I will be the heroine." But I couldn't seem to think of a title for this play.

There were three hooks on the wall, on one hung a black uniform and white apron, waiting for me. I hung up my hat and went downstairs.

Mrs. Richards did not look like a cook at all. Cooks are meant to be jolly and plump from tasting all their baking. They are meant to have laugh wrinkles and bright red cheeks from bending over the roast beef or the steamed pudding. They were not meant to be tall and thin with a deep voice and only frown lines on their faces. I thought she probably wasn't a very good cook. I hoped I wouldn't starve.

Mrs. Richards barked that my duties would begin at six in the morning, *in uniform.* "And if it's too big, you'll pin it." I was to stoke the fire in the wood stove first thing, so the master and mistress could bathe in warm water. *"And you'll carry it to their room without spilling a drop, girl."* Miss Marilyn, she told me, is seventeen years old and sleeps late. "You'll take her water up when she rings for it." There was a row of bells above the kitchen door, each with a sign beneath that named a different room in the house. I was to run to the room that rang. Fast.

She showed me the pantry — *"which I keep locked, don't get any ideas"* — the scullery, dining room and sitting room. The sitting room was so crowded with pictures and furniture and bric-a-brac you could hardly move in it. All that curly iron work around the fireplace would have to be dusted and washed. By me. The brass fire screen, in the shape of a peacock with its tail spread out, would have to be kept shiny. By me. All those doilies would have to be bleached, blued, starched and ironed. By me. The gas chandelier had about a million pieces of glass hanging down. Just the thought of cleaning that room made me tired.

The next morning began at running speed and only got faster throughout the day. I was to make the beds and clean the bedrooms and wait at table. I was in charge of cleaning up in the scullery — dishes three times a day. I was to run errands for Mrs. Richards and lay the fires and clean the grates and lamp chimneys and polish the silver and dust all six sitting room clocks that tick-tocked life away. I was to dust the figurines on the mantel and the piano and the tables and all the bleedin' pictures and paintings hung all around the house and propped up on tables and shelves. The windows and the brass were to be polished to perfection. And there were peas to shell, beets to scrub, carrots and potatoes from the kitchen garden to peel. Once a week there was laundry and ironing. If the mending was finished by nine o'clock at night, I could go to bed.

"What about school? And church?" I asked.

"We'll see how quick you are, girl, and if there's time."

"But at the Home . . . Matron said — "

"*Girl!*" she snapped. "I said we'll see. Now attend to the duties you were hired for!" And that was the end of that.

Miss Marilyn goes to parties a lot. She sleeps late, so when she rings, I have to stop what I'm doing to carry up her breakfast on a tray and heat her bath water. No matter what I'm doing later, if she wants a dress ironed, or her hairpins fetched, or her mirror held up so she can see the back of her head, I stop that chore and go to her.

By the end of my first week, I could hardly feel the blisters on my hands and feet, hardly hear the "*hurry up, girl,*" hardly notice how Miss Marilyn talks to me like I'm a bad dog. I was that tired. But no matter how tired I was, the fighting always woke me up, put me on alert.

Almost every night after dinner, the master and missus had what she called "a discussion". They argued. Their voices got louder and louder. Sometimes they threw dishes. It ended when the doors slammed, which meant they'd gone out or to bed. I was grateful that the fights were usually in the dining room, not the sitting room. There were fewer things for them to break and for me to clean up.

One morning after I'd put away the master's shaving things, made the bed and swept the carpet in the big bedroom, I was dusting a large, round picture. The glass was rounded like a bubble, instead of flat, and the frame was varnished dark wood. Inside was a wreath of strange little flowers. They were brown, gold and white and had little beads here and there. It took me a few minutes to realize what I was looking at. The flowers were woven out of hair, like what's left in your brush in the morning! I was staring at them so hard I didn't hear the missus come in.

"*Here* now! What do you mean by standing and gawking at my mourning wreath!" I whirled around, and my feather duster caught a figurine on the table. It smashed into a million pieces. The missus flew across the room and slapped my face.

After all the fighting and breaking that she does herself, you wouldn't think she'd miss a little blue china girl holding a blue china dog, but she was furious.

"Clumsy! Snoop! What are you thinking?"

"I beg your pardon, missus. I've never seen . . . I didn't mean . . ."

"You Home Children are all alike. The last one was the same. Sneaky, cheeky! And a thief, too! Clean up this instant. You'll pay for that from your wages."

I was too shocked to cry. I knelt and swept the china bits off the rug, into the metal dust pan, and carried it to the kitchen.

"You're all the same, you English brats," said Mrs. Richards. "They only get you, 'cause you're cheap. If it was up to me, I wouldn't have nothing but Canadian-born help."

The thing is, when you're very, very tired, it's hard to think about escape. All you want to do is get through the day and get upstairs even if it is an oven, and be alone. Just be still and be away from them all. I thought about writing my friends who came out to Canada with me, but that would mean asking Mrs. Richards how to get stamps and paper and it was too much. I thought about what they told us at the Home in England, that this would be a way for us to begin again. I thought about Matron at the Home in Peterborough. "We'll send around an inspector to see you," she'd said. But when? How long would I have to wait?

Some nights I'd lie awake and listen to the train whistle in the distance and pretend that I was on it. Pierre Paul, the lumberjack I'd met on the train from Québec would be on it, too, and we would ride all over the whole country and he would give me maple sugar candy and tell stories that I could easily make into plays. Whenever the train stopped, we'd see Tim, my best friend from London, and me and Tim would perform the plays just like we used to do when we were little and Dad wasn't dead and before I had to go to live in the Home. And the plays would be grand, and people would come from miles around to see us. But mostly, I was too tired to imagine. I didn't even have the energy to unpack my trunk.

I'd been there one month exactly when it all happened. After a concert at the Massey Music Hall one afternoon, the missus brought three ladies home for tea. The first one through the door had a pinched face and wore a purple hat with purple feathers. In my head I called her *Miss Feathers.* The second wore more brooches, rings and pendants than Queen Victoria herself. *Mrs. Jewels.* The last one was slow and old and had a face like a nice dried apple. Her cane had a silver duck head for a handle. *Madam Duck Handle.*

When I carried the silver tray into the sitting room, Miss Feathers was speaking. "I've sent mine back," she declared, "and I'll never get another. It's a wonder I wasn't murdered in my bed!" I set down the tray and went to stand by the door, as ordered, in case I was needed.

"It's true. The money saved by hiring a Home Child is soon lost in what they steal and break!" said Mrs. Jewels. "Mark my words, they'll be the ruin of the upper class of Toronto. The thing is, they've no character, no backbone. That's why they're *in* the lower class to begin with." She sipped her tea and helped herself to another pastry that I'd made that morning. "And how is yours getting on, my dear?"

"She's small," said my mistress, "and slow. One day I found her snooping in my bedroom. She broke a little figurine, something my dear, departed mother gave me." She sighed. "It's a trial, isn't it?"

"You *see*? I hope you punished her," said Miss Feathers.

Madam Duck Handle suddenly rapped her cane on the floor. "Forgive an old woman," she said, "but I don't believe that Home Children are any worse than others. Isn't all this talk a bit exaggerated? Isn't it just because they're different from us that people don't like them? They're indeed from a lower class, and their English is hard to understand, but really, that doesn't make them criminals!"

"You're too soft. What I know is from experience and from what I read. Even the newspapers are against them, my dear," replied Mrs. Jewels. "Send them back where they came from, I say."

Just then Miss Marilyn entered the room.

"Ah!" cooed Miss Feathers. "Now here's a young lady we can be proud of. How lovely your dress is!"

Miss Marilyn blushed and flapped her eyelashes. She didn't say who had stayed up half the night ironin' the bleedin' dress.

"Aren't you afraid," Miss Feathers continued, "that your Home Girl might influence, might contaminate your lovely daughter?"

"Oh, I know how to deal with servants," Miss Marilyn said, taking a little custard tart. "Servants aren't like us. They don't think like us at all. They don't have the same wants and needs as we have, do they mother?"

"She's fortunate to be here at all, dear," her mother said.

Miss Marilyn took a second tart. "Why, I've read Mr. Dickens' stories. Goodness, she could be selling matches on a street corner in the rain or working in a ribbon factory fourteen hours a day. We've done her a great service by having her here at all!"

Mrs. Jewels laughed. "Yes, I suppose that's one way to

look at it. We're providing a community service, doing a good deed by allowing them to work for us. How clever you are, Marilyn, dear. I'd never have thought of that."

I couldn't bear to hear another word and left the room, pretending that I needed to bring in more sweets. My cheeks burned; my heart was broken.

This isn't what I thought Canada would be like. The only Canadian I ever saw in London was Miss Pauline Johnson when she came to perform her poems in the theatre. She was beautiful and wonderful and she was a true Indian princess and when she told about Canada it wasn't about dead people's hair in picture frames and people being mean. It was about people being free and loving the land and being brave.

The people at the Home in London said that if we went to Canada we'd be welcomed and that the Canadians *wanted* us to come.

But what happened? And what could I do now? The agreement with the Home was that I stay here until age fourteen. My wages went directly to the Home until then. I was stuck for two years more, without a penny to my name. But after that, God help me, I'll find my old friend Tim and we'll do our plays and we'll go and find Miss Pauline John-son's *real* Canada.

That night I was left alone to clean the kitchen and scullery. It was late; I was tired. I poured hot water and soap into the basin to wash the mountain of dishes.

Mrs. Richards was in bed with a headache. Miss Marilyn was at a concert. The missus had gone to bed right after the usual Saturday night fight with her husband. The master had gone out. Now he was back. Standing in the scullery. Drunk.

He smelled bad. Worse than when Dad had gone out for a wee nip. Much worse. "You've been here a few weeks now," he said.

"Yessir."

"You haven't seen the city yet."

"No, sir."

"How about a little kiss, girl? Maybe later I could show you the city."

"No, sir," I said. "I don't think that would be proper." My heart raced. A lump clogged up my throat.

"Come on, girl. Just a little kiss." He came toward me fast then, fumbling with his trouser buttons with one hand and reaching out for me with his other hand. Before I could think, I picked up that dishpan full of hot soapy water and threw it at him. Then I was running up the stairs as fast as I could. He followed close, cursing and yelling. I was terrified, not tired now, no, just get . . . no! If I went to my room, I'd be trapped! He was right behind me. I turned, put my head down and pushed with all my might. He fell backward down the stairs, hollering and grabbing for me. In no time I was out the front door, running. When I heard the train whistle I turned and ran toward it.

I ran and ran down the streets, into the hot summer night. When I reached the railway tracks I plopped down in the ditch. I could hear three sounds: my heart thumping, my breath racing, and the crickets chirping in the grass. *Where could I go?*

What pulled me up out of the tall ditch grass and onto my feet wasn't the whistle of the next train. It was red rage.

How *dare* she slap my face! How *dare* she never say my name! How *dare* they say I have no backbone! *How dare he come after me like that!* Never. Never. Never. I shall never return to that house.

Even though my legs were shaking, I started to walk. To march. Left-right, left-right. My boots crunched hard against the gravel between the railway ties. I shall walk back to Peterborough. I shall *march* back and tell Matron to find me another place. If it takes me a week or a month or a year, I'll get there. I'll find the real Canada. And I shall begin again.

Magic, Pure Magic

The Story of Raymond Munro's
First Solo Flight

〜 by Margaret Florczak

The black tarmac of the aerodrome was soft under the hot August sun, and sixteen-year-old Raymond Munro prodded a bubble of tar with the toe of his shoe while Mr. Gillies filled out the log book. It was the summer of 1937, the 1929 de Havilland Gypsy Moth biplane was back in its hangar and Raymond's flying lesson had ended with a perfect three point landing.

"You're about the youngest kid I've given lessons to, son."

"Is that right, sir?"

"Sure is." Fred Gillies, owner of the Dufferin Flying Service, finished making the journal entry. The Flying Service consisted of several planes: the Moth, an old Aeronca-C, and a Taylor Cub to mention just three. Fred and some of the hired help gave flying lessons when they weren't busy transporting people and goods up north. The Flying Service operated out of Barker Airfield, several dusty acres with a landing strip and a couple of hangars along the highway just outside Toronto. He added, "I'll bet your dad's pretty proud of you."

Raymond cleared his throat. "When do you figure I'll be ready for my solo flight?"

"Next time out," Gillies said decisively, spat on the tarmac and added, "bring your dad over sometime. I'd like to meet him."

"Sure thing, sir! Thank you, sir!" Raymond was glad his father wasn't here. His father wouldn't tolerate spitting even if Mr. Gillies did own the airfield.

"A pilot! You're going to be a real pilot?" Roy could hardly believe his brother's news.

"You bet! Like Clark Gable. I'll be navigating through fog and ice, making emergency landings, maybe even have to crash land in the jungle."

"You've got that part right — the crash landing," Roy laughed. At eighteen, he was well aware of his younger brother's reckless ways.

"Oh, you're jealous," Raymond said.

"Honestly, you can hardly come into our room without hitting your head on the door frame, or tripping over your feet."

"That's because I'm growing and it's hard to keep everything coordinated."

"It's because you're in such a heck of a hurry you don't look where you're going."

"Oh, come on, Roy, what's banging my head got to do with anything?"

"Well, it's got to do with how dangerous I think it is for you to be flying," Roy said candidly. "I think we ought to talk to father about this. What if something happens to you?"

"You're just like dad. He thinks I'm too much of a klutz to learn to fly without killing myself," Raymond complained irritably. "Won't you two be surprised when I get my pilot's license!"

Roy looked doubtful. "What if we're right?"

"Oh, come on, Roy, haven't you ever wished you could fly? It's magic, up there away from everyone and everything, pure magic. And my next flight," Raymond continued, "I'm going solo, flying the plane all by myself."

"Look, Raymond, I just think dad should know."

"You can't spoil this for me now. It's amazing fun. Look, I'll tell you what — come with me on my solo flight."

Roy's eyes lit up. "Could I?"

"Sure. But only if you don't tell dad."

Roy narrowed his eyes while he thought about this. "You're right. He'd never let us both risk our necks — not with you at the controls!"

Raymond breathed a sigh of relief. He had dreamed of

being a pilot all his life, reading up on airplanes, making models from kits and learning all he could about Canadian bush pilots. From his home on Sherbourne Street, it was eight miles to Barker Field where he worked to earn his flying lessons. He could have taken a streetcar part of the way, but instead, he walked to save the nickel fare. Weeks ago, when he had folded his legs into the cockpit of the Moth for his first lesson, Raymond sensed that he was about to begin the adventure of his life. As the biplane scooted over the runway, gathered speed and lifted off into the blue sky, Raymond could hear his pulse throbbing above the roar of the engine and feel tears stinging his eyes. High above the earth, free as he had never been before, this was where he belonged.

During his flying lessons, Raymond found he was assigned the Aeronca-C, a plane that was shaped liked a bathtub, with a cramped cockpit, and a heavy undercarriage. He soon learned that if the wind or temperature wasn't just right the temperamental beast might not even achieve lift-off. It took a long time to earn his lessons, and it was bitterly disappointing to spend most of his time just trying to get the Aeronca off the ground. One day, he heard a man tell Mr. Gillies not to insult him by trying to sell him lessons in that old air knocker. Raymond knew he couldn't talk to Mr. Gillies in the same manner. He might never get another lesson if he did. But after washing down a bi-plane and sweeping the length of a huge hangar, Raymond decided he wouldn't be disappointed again. He would speak up. When he'd finished neatly coiling the hose on its holder and put the rags away in the bin, he went over to where Mr. Gillies was oiling some engine parts.

"Mr. Gillies," Raymond shuffled his feet in the dust by the hangar.

"What is it, Raymond?" Mr. Gillies squinted while he aimed the long thin nozzle of an oil can at a bearing.

"Well, sir, they give me that old tub to fly, did you know that, sir?" Raymond hooked his thumbs in his pockets.

"Uh-huh. What about it, son?"

"Well, sir, that old tub just doesn't always get up like she should. She wobbles a fair bit."

Raymond suddenly remembered what his dad said when he put his hands, even his thumbs in his pockets. *Don't you go sassing me, boy!* Raymond looked at Mr. Gillies, but he didn't seem to mind. All the same, Raymond took his thumbs out of his pockets.

"She's unsteady, is she?" Mr. Gillies stood up and wiped the end of the nozzle and then his hands with an old oily rag.

"Yes, sir."

"Hmmm. Well, tell you what. How about we switch you to the Taylor Cub?"

"That'd be fine, Mr. Gillies, just fine!"

The morning of the solo flight, the Munro brothers woke just as the sun was nudging the houses on Sherbourne Street. Because they needed to be at the field as early as possible, Roy splurged and paid for the streetcar. By 7 a.m. they were already settled in their seats, feeling how absolutely satisfactory it was to be brothers.

"Look, Roy, I'm not really supposed to take anyone up with me," Raymond admitted as they stepped down from the streetcar and headed out across the fields. "It's okay; but we have to be careful."

"What'll happen if we're found out?"

"Oh, Gillies will get a little hot around the collar, that's all," Raymond shrugged. He knew it was wrong to take a passenger when he didn't have his license. If he got caught, he'd be in big trouble. He began to whistle.

The boys walked in silence, Raymond thinking of how to smuggle Roy onto the plane, and Roy thinking uneasily that there was undoubtedly something his brother hadn't told him. But Roy wanted so badly to go flying: Raymond wasn't the only Munro who was crazy about aeronautics. Roy sighed. It was just like his little brother to go taking lessons without dad's permission.

"Hey, don't worry!" Raymond clapped him on the back. "I've got it all figured out." After much discussion, they agreed on a plan.

"So I'll cut across the airfield, where the rail fence is, and hide there," confirmed Roy.

"Right. And I'll come over and pick you up, taxiing the plane between you and the airstrip. Just run along beside me, and keep low when you jump in."

"All right!"

Just outside the airstrip, before parting company, the boys ate their lunch.

"Here, have a sandwich," Raymond offered his brother, unwrapping the waxed paper from a pink blob.

"What is it?" asked Roy nervously.

"Tomato sandwiches."

"Tomato sandwiches?" Roy peered closely at the mushy red mass his brother held out to him. "That doesn't look like tomato sandwiches."

"Well, they got a little beat up in my pocket."

Roy raised his eyebrows, and gingerly took one. He was too hungry to refuse. "I hope you've at least got some water to wash them down with."

"As soon as we get to the gas pumps."

"The gas pumps?"

"Yeah. They've got a water hose over there."

"The one they use to fill radiators? The water will taste of rubber and smell like gasoline."

"The perfect accompaniment for these sandwiches," grinned Raymond.

Roy playfully swatted his brother and the boys began laughing and jabbing each other, making dire threats between pounces. Finally, they settled down to lunch.

"Better head on out," Raymond said, seeing the sun high in the sky.

He had intended to take Roy up in the Gypsy Moth. It handled nicely and had two seats, one behind the other. But to his dismay, the only plane left in the hangars was the old tub. Raymond looked around. Gillies and the mechanic were up to their elbows in grease under an engine.

"Hey, Raymond," Mr. Gillies lugged on a wrench and then pushed his cap up on his forehead and said, "I guess you'll have to wait awhile for that solo flight."

"Oh, heck, I'll be okay, Mr. Gillies. You know I can handle her."

"I thought you'd want to take the moth. Jack'll have her back this afternoon, if you want to wait."

Raymond looked over to where Roy was crouched in his hiding place beside the old rail fence. "Oh, shucks, that's okay. I don't mind taking the tub. I just want to get it over with."

Gillies looked doubtful. Oil dripped from the engine onto his forehead. Wiping his face with a rag, he nodded, "Okay. Just be careful, Raymond."

"Yes, sir. You bet." Raymond nodded and waved and backed away toward the hangar.

"And Raymond?"

"Yes, sir?"

"I'll be keeping an eye on you."

Once at the Aeronca, Raymond fired it up. As he passed

the mechanic's shed, he waved nonchalantly. Gillies gave him a salute with his wrench and Raymond continued to guide the clumsy craft down the field, checking the instrumentation on the way. Slowly, he taxied past the fence where his brother lay waiting. The plane rocked when Roy leapt up and squeezed himself into the cockpit beside Raymond.

"Whoa! Is this tub safe to fly in?" asked Roy as he did up the safety harness.

"What are you calling a tub? You want a plane ride or don't you?" snapped Raymond.

Roy had been half-kidding, but now he began to feel anxious.

"Do your seat belt up and watch for approaching hazards!"

"Watch for what? Oh, you're just joking." Roy was not amused.

Sweat formed on his forehead, as Raymond opened the throttle. The plane slowly responded. He suddenly remembered that the Aeronca built up speed over distance, and he had picked Roy up near the end of the runway. This meant that the Aeronca had hardly any distance to get airborne. "Oh, no," he groaned.

"Everything's all right, isn't it, Raymond?"

Without replying, Raymond leaned forward, willing the plane to lift over the fence that separated the airfield from the highway.

"That fence is getting awful close, Raymond. And look at those telephone wires!"

Raymond didn't have to look. He knew this part of the ride by heart. Telephone poles stretched along the edge of the road. Beyond that, another fence sagged in front of a cluster of old farm buildings. The Aeronca should have been well above all of this; instead, it clung stubbornly to the runway.

Raymond pulled back on the stick and the tub swayed, hesitated, then lifted over the fence. But the heavy air-knocker didn't have sufficient speed to keep it airborne. Seeing this, Raymond jerked the stick back down, dropping the Aeronca under the telephone wires.

"Oh, no! We're in the middle of the road! Raymond! Do something!"

Raymond stared down at the center line of the highway. A roadster squealed to a halt, and a coupe sped by, narrowly avoiding them. Horns blared. An angry driver shook his fist and swore at the plane. Raymond knew that if Gillies was watching, he was doing the same thing.

As the plane hit, the landing gear struck the pavement, the impact bouncing the plane up over the wire fence on the other side of the highway. Still airborne, the plane bungled forward, heading straight into some mushroom sheds. Raymond pulled back on the stick as hard as he could. The plane fumbled upward, the engine faltered, the wings dipped.

"Look out!" Roy hollered, grabbing the stick.

"What are you doing! Stop it! Let go!" Raymond yelled, pushing him away. Roy's foot flew up, hitting the stick, shoving it forward. In horror the boys saw the nose of the Aeronca slowly shift downward.

The propeller just cleared the roof of the first shed. With a sickening grinding and chopping sound, the wheels touched down, rolling over the dried, curled-up shingles. It seemed to take forever for the plane to roll up one side of the roof and coast down the other, gathering speed. As they hurtled over the edge, the old bath tub sailed gracefully upward, into the air.

"Don't ever touch that stick. If you ever do that again — " Raymond scolded.

"I just saved our lives," Roy retorted, "We didn't have enough speed to get over those sheds. If we hadn't landed *on* them, we'd have crashed *into* them. So don't tell me what to do, Mr. Hot Shot Pilot."

The frightened boys flew in silence for awhile, collecting their thoughts.

"What now?" Roy asked, well aware that this had turned into another of Raymond's escapades.

"Are you okay?" Raymond asked.

"Just scared. Why?"

"Because I have to let you off away from the airstrip. It'll mean a longer walk home for you."

"I don't care. It's all my fault for agreeing to come. I knew better."

"Too bad it turned into such a disaster."

"Not really. Look at us — we're flying! You're right, Raymond. Even though I know it's all about aerodynamic principles, it feels like magic, pure magic."

"Hmmm. So you're somewhat enjoying this?"

"Somewhat," Roy grinned.

"Guess we'll have to land in that old field where we used to have Boy Scout camp."

"Beside the Rouge River?"

"Yeah."

At the field, they were greeted by a herd of cows. Raymond flew low over the animals while Roy leaned out, waving his hat and yelling at them. The boys laughed as the cows plodded away from the aircraft, tails swishing. Raymond set the plane down gently.

"Life with you is always an adventure, little brother," Roy grinned as he said goodbye.

"Watch out for those cow-pies."

On his way back to the airfield, Raymond fought with his conscience. He had taken off his hat and jacket and buckled them into the passenger seat after Roy'd left. He had no trouble landing. As he brought the plane in, Gillies strode out to meet him.

"What on earth do you think you're doing? You know you're not allowed to have a passenger up there with you!"

"What passenger?" Raymond countered.

Gillies marched around the plane and saw the jacket and hat strapped into the seat. He slapped his palm on the plane in disgust. "That doesn't fool me for a second!" he snapped. "Don't you try pulling the wool over my eyes, no sir. I know what I saw," he leaned forward, his sour breath warm on Raymond's scarlet face, "and what I saw was you up there with a passenger."

Raymond lowered his eyes and stuck to his story. Gillies got so angry that little drops of spittle formed around his words. Finally, in disgust, he unstrapped the clothing and flung it at Raymond. "If you're going to stand there and tell me bare-faced lies, you can take your jacket and your cap and get off this airfield and don't you ever set foot on it again. Have I made myself clear?"

"Yes, sir," Raymond said sadly.

He left the airfield knowing that Mr. Gillies couldn't prove a thing against him. He had saved his flying career. But he could never come back to Barker Field, or to his job at Dufferin Flying Service. And he would never hear praise from Mr. Gillies, ever again. He had ruined everything. He was sick at heart.

It was late at night when he climbed up onto the porch of the house on Sherbourne Street and quietly eased the screen door open.

"Be careful. You'll wake mom and pop."

"Geez, Roy, you scared me half to death."

"Yeah, well, that makes us even."

"You got home all right?"

"No problem. How was Gillies?"

"Madder than a dog three feet from a henhouse and tied up on two feet of rope."

The boys sat in silence on the big wicker chairs.

Raymond sighed heavily. "What am I going to do, Roy? Flying is my whole life, and Mr. Gillies never wants to see me again as long as he lives."

"Did he say that?"

"Might as well have."

"Look, Raymond, there's something I have to tell you."

"Not now, okay, Roy?" Raymond smelled cigar smoke, and glanced up. "Dad!"

"Good evening boys. You didn't come and say good-night, Raymond."

"Gosh, sir, I didn't know you were still up."

"You got home awful late. Had your mother worried." The red tip of his cigar glowed eerily in the night. Raymond swung his long legs back and forth. Roy examined his fingertips in the dark. "Your brother told me about the trouble today."

Raymond swung around and glared accusingly at his brother before telling his father: "You don't have to worry about me taking any more flying lessons, sir. Mr. Gillies will never let me set foot on his airfield again."

"Hmm. That's too bad. Seems to me this Gillies is a pretty good chap. Roy told me you're making progress. Already soloed."

Raymond nodded numbly in the darkness.

"Yes sir." His father despised disobedience, and his punishments were severe.

Mr. Munro drew deeply on his cigar, the mellow smoke filling the small porch. "My boys aren't quitters," he said sternly.

Raymond sighed, and lowered his head to hide his tears.

But his father continued. "Do you understand, son?"

Raymond nodded, wiping his sleeve across his eyes in the dark.

"Finish your lessons, son, but on one condition: you are not to endanger your brother or any one else. Have I made myself clear?"

Raymond looked up in disbelief. "I think so, yes, sir!" he said.

"Well, then, g'night, boys."

"G'night, dad."

"Good night, sir."

As soon as the boys heard the bedroom door close, they burst out in a suppressed whoop of joy. Then Raymond grabbed his brother. "You rat! you dirty rat," he exclaimed, pushing Roy off his chair. There was a loud thump as Roy hit the porch.

"Everything all right out there?"

"Fine, dad." Raymond put out a hand and helped his brother up.

"Want to go for a walk?" asked Roy.

"Can't. Have to get up early tomorrow."

Raymond was at the airport before the offices opened. He waited until Gillies had poured a coffee and settled into his chair before knocking on the door.

"What do you want?" Gillies growled.

"To apologize, sir, and explain." Raymond began to sit down.

"Stand up!" Gillies snapped.

"Yes, sir!" Raymond finished his well-rehearsed speech on his feet. Gillies drained his coffee, a plane droned in the distance. Crickets chirped just outside the door. Sweat dampened Raymond's brow. Still, Gillies said nothing, but he picked up his goggles and grabbed his jacket off the hook by the door.

"Follow me."

Raymond hurried to keep up as Gillies marched over to the Moth's hangar and climbed into the open cockpit.

"Get in," Gillies ordered, indicating the seat behind him. His lips pressed tightly together, he fired her up and taxied down the runway. Raymond was still strapping his harness on, the wind ruffling his hair, as they left the tarmac. He anxiously waited for Mr. Gillies to speak. But Gillies didn't say a word.

Instead, he took the plane straight up, higher than Raymond had ever been before. For the first time in his flying career, Raymond felt uncomfortable. Sweat moistened his palms. His breakfast sat in an uneasy lump in his stomach. Without warning, Gillies plunged them into a rapid figure eight, rolling the plane upside down hundreds of feet in the air. Houses and fields spun dizzily beneath them. Just before it seemed the plane must surely crash, Gillies pulled up. They leveled out briefly, then shot straight up.

Once again, Gillies dove, hurtling toward the earth. Raymond felt his breakfast shift unpleasantly upward. As the ground zoomed perilously near, Raymond gripped the dashboard, willing his food to stay down. Finally, he felt the plane lift and wheel away. Barely had he caught his breath and brought his breakfast back into the area of his intestinal cavity when Gillies plunged into a rapid series of loop-the-loops. Raymond's breakfast heaved between his stomach and his throat. Once more the plane rushed to meet the ground, swirling houses and fields around. Raymond felt the blood from his face drain down to his stomach where his breakfast heaved like a volcano. Gillies glanced over at Raymond and burst out laughing.

Safely landed, Raymond unfolded his jelly-like legs, and stood tremulously on solid ground. Mr. Gillies lost no time launching into an angry tirade.

"I ought to kick you off this field forever. I ought to report you for taking a passenger up, and never give you another lesson as long as you live. I ought to—"

Gillies shoved his goggles back on his forehead and looked at the shame-faced boy. "Ah, heck. I'll tell you this much, kid. It takes courage to make a good flier, and what you did today, telling the truth, that was courageous." He offered Raymond his hand. Raymond gripped it in as firm a handshake as he could manage.

"Now get out of here and don't come back till Monday. I've got work to do."

Raymond sprinted for the bushes behind the hangar. He leaned into a clump of red maple maple and let his breakfast erupt. When his stomach was completely empty, he washed up at the gas pumps and headed for home. He'd had a long night, a rough day, and he was starving.

Historical Notes & Author Biographies

✑ GIFT OF THE OLD WIVES (page 14)

In Saskatchewan, in the early 1800s, a great fire swept across the plains, driving the bison westward in search of food. The popular story goes that a Cree tribe from Qu'Appelle followed the bison, finding them in enemy Blackfoot territory near a large lake south-west of what is now Moose Jaw.

After the Cree people had secured meat to take back to Qu'Appelle, they began their journey home but soon came upon Blackfoot horsemen who shot a few arrows, then disappeared. The Cree people knew that the Blackfoot — a stronger tribe than they — would return at dawn to wage battle.

An old Cree woman went to the chief and offered to keep the fires burning, so that the Blackfoot would take their time in coming, thinking that the camp was settled. By the time the attack began, the rest of the Cree tribe would have escaped.

The chief accepted the plan and led the tribe to safety while all night long, old women heaped the campfires with bison chips. When the Blackfoot arrived in the morning, all they found were a few old wives wrapped in blankets, whom they killed. The rest of the Cree tribe escaped safely.

The lake was named Old Wives' Lake in honour of these brave old women. In the 1860s, the lake was renamed Lake Johnstone after an Englishman who hunted there, but public pressure restored its original name in 1953. It is said that on windy nights, one can hear mocking laughter from an island in the lake, the old Cree women continuing to enjoy the trick they played on their enemy.

BEVERLEY BRENNA is the author of two junior novels — *The Keeper of the Trees* and *Spider Summer* — and a picture book — *Daddy Longlegs at Birch Lane*. Her young adult short stories include "Higher Ground," about Nellie McClung, which has appeared in several anthologies and textbooks, and she also publishes poetry and short fiction for adults. Beverley lives on an acreage with her husband and three children, and teaches in nearby Saskatoon, Saskatchewan.

ᔧ— FIRST ENCOUNTER (page 29)

At the very beginning of the nineteenth century, the North-West Company decided to find out whether it was feasible to pursue their fur business west of the Rocky Mountains. To that end, they sent Simon Fraser on an expedition which resulted, amongst other things, in the discovery of the river that bears his name, and the founding of a number of fur posts, including the one at the southern tip of Stuart Lake, Fort St. James.

The Company needed several assurances before they would risk an expansion into such a wilderness. First, they had to be sure of a good supply of fur-bearing animals, particularly beaver. Second, they wanted to find a route to the Pacific to simplify and speed up the shipping of the furs. Third, no fur post was ever set up unless there was a good supply of a staple food in the area; freight was much too expensive to consider sending a year's food for the employees on the annual supply train.

Fraser found all these things. The fort he established on Stuart

Lake is still there, flying the flag of the Hudson's Bay Company, which amalgamated with the North-West Company in 1821. The country he found reminded him of his native Scotland, so he called it New Caledonia. It was a huge area that encompassed modern B.C., and extended down to the border of Washington and Oregon. Until the middle of the nineteenth century, the fur post on Stuart Lake was the administrative centre of the whole region.

The moments of contact between Europeans and indigenous peoples in North America often went unrecorded. Where they were set down, it was usually by the Europeans. Their accounts naturally reflect their own points of view and cannot be relied upon to give the whole story. The Carrier people of the interior of B.C. no doubt had a version of the encounter between Chief Kwah and Fraser's men in their oral tradition, but their language had no written form until the late nineteenth century when an Oblate priest at Fort St. James, called Father A.G. Morice, invented a phonetic alphabet for the Carrier language.

In his *The History of the Northern Interior of British Columbia*, Father Morice tells about this encounter. Probably he got some of his information from the Carrier people in his congregation, but this would have been more than sixty years after the event. Father Morice did not like the Hudson's Bay Company and always portrayed its employees in the most unflattering terms. At the same time, he had a paternalistic attitude to the native people, and regarded them as little more than children. This did not make for unbiased accounts either!

With this sort of source material, I make no apology for invention. Father Morice provided a framework, but I made up a number of the incidents and some of the characters, although I like to think they are all plausible. Fraser, McDougall, the interpreter, Jean-Baptiste Boucher, Chief Kwah and Toeyen actually lived in the harsh conditions of the "Siberia of the fur trade." The fur traders could not have flourished or even survived without the cooperation and support of the indigenous people, who had ten thousand years' worth of knowledge and expertise certainly not shared by the Europeans. It seems only fair that a story about the first time the two groups met each other should represent both equally, and acknowledge their common humanity while recognizing that their different backgrounds must inevitably have led to misunderstandings and misconceptions.

MARGARET THOMPSON is the author of the young adult historical novel *Eyewitness,* winner of the B.C. 2000 Book Award and the "Our Choice" Award. She has also published *Squaring the Round,* a book of poetry and prose about the early days of Fort St. James, and *Hide and Seek,* a collection of short stories for adults. One of her essays, "Still Life," is included in an anthology of West Coast writers, *An Ear to the Ground,* published in Seattle. A number of her poems and creative non-fiction pieces have appeared in literary magazines. Margaret Thompson now lives in Victoria, B.C.

∽ COURAGE, MARGUERITE (page 47)

By 1661 the French population of Québec, then Nouvelle France, numbered fewer than 2,500 people. King Louis XIV of France, with the help of Minister Colbert, decided to remedy the situation by taking steps to accelerate the growth of the populace.

The king's treasury paid a price of ten livres per head to people hired to find young, virtuous women who would consent to go to Nouvelle France for the purpose of marrying and producing a family. Because the money came from the king's treasury the young women were given the name *filles du roi.* Sixty livres were paid for the transport and a dowry of 30 livres was to be given to each young woman upon marrying. By 1664 the dowry had been increased to 50 livres. Taking into account that a common laborer would work a year to make that amount of money, this was a considerable sum for a young, single woman. As well, each girl received a trousseau consisting of articles she would need in her new life, such as a pair of scissors, pins and needles. For a young woman with no prospects, orphans or widows left without means, New France offered an adventure and the possibility of a better, though not easier, life.

Between 1663 and 1673, 774 young women, many of them recruited from orphanages such as L'Hôpital Général and its two satellite institutions, La Salpêtrière and La Santé, crossed the Atlantic. Although life in the orphanages was not easy, it in no way prepared them, some as young as twelve, for the difficulties they would face during the crossing and once they reached the new world.

The trip, lasting from two to three months depending on the weather, was not a pleasure cruise. Breakfast was meat, cheese, and hard tack — a hard biscuit made with flour and water, that when cooked and stored properly could last for months. Supper consisted of hard tack and not much else each day for the length of the journey. The women accompanying the *filles du roi* were not always gentle and some of them helped themselves to the goods in the girls' trousseaus.

The boats were small, crowded, and unsanitary — no *Titanics* or *Queen Marys*. Bathrooms as we know them did not exist. During one crossing, a ship sank. Its passengers were rescued by another ship travelling with them. That vessel, with its provisions for one crew and passengers, cared for the crews and passengers of two ships for the rest of the journey. It is a miracle so few died during these transports.

Upon arriving at Québec, the first of three stops, *les filles* were conducted to a building where they were able to meet some of the men looking for wives. Many were chosen and married within hours. Those not chosen got back on the boat and continued up-river to Trois Rivières and Montréal, leading to the still popular saying that the prettiest girls come from Québec City.

Marguerite's fear of and prejudice towards the Amerindians was generally shared by the invading population.

At the time of Marguerite's journey there was a large, non-migratory population of beluga whales in the St. Lawrence River. By 1900 this population was estimated to be approximately 5,000. The descendants of this group of whales still swim in the same area, though their range is smaller and the herd has been reduced to around 500, the result of a whaling industry that stopped hunting belugas only in the mid-1900s, and the ravages of industrial pollution.

SUSAN LEE was born in Ontario. Her short story "Bridges" was included in the Thistledown Press young adult anthology *Notes Across the Aisle.* She has published poetry for children in *Carkner's Corners,* an American writers' review. Susan is also a graduate of The Ontario College of Art and has exhibited her visual work in Ontario, Québec and New York City. She lives outside Montréal, Québec with her husband and two children, their two cats, two horses and a pony.

ᐂ— THE LITTLE IRON HORSE (page 57)

The Canadian Horse is a little known national treasure. It traces its ancestry to the foundation stock originally shipped to New France by King Louis XIV. In the late 1600s, the King sent two stallions and twenty mares from the royal stables to start a herd in the North American colony. For hundreds of years, the French horses multiplied with very little influence from outside breeds and they eventually developed into their own distinct breed — the Canadian Horse or *cheval canadien.*

Generally these horses are black. They stand 14–16 hands high and weigh from 1,000 to 1,400 pounds. Their appearance is characterized by finely chiselled heads, arched necks and thick, long, wavy manes and tails. They are renowned for their kind, sensible, sociable nature, their intelligence and their willingness to please.

In the mid-1800s there were approximately 150,000 Canadian Horses throughout North America. Recognized as a sound general utility animal, these horses had outstanding qualities of strength, willingness to please and small food requirements; they were widely used for crossbreeding purposes, to improve the strength and hardiness of other breeds. The Canadian Horse helped found several North American breeds, including the Morgan, Tennessee Walking Horse, Standardbred and American Saddlebred. Increasingly, however, Canadian Horses were exported: for use in the Boer War, on sugar plantations in the West Indies and to the United States for use on stage lines and in the Civil War. With the advent of mechanized farm equipment in Canada, their numbers dwindled rapidly and the breed almost became extinct.

By the 1960s there were fewer than 400 Canadian Horses left. Ten years later, the threat to Canada's national breed had been recognized and efforts were begun by diligent breeders to bring it back. The breed is slowly gaining in popularity and today numbers over 2,500.

Because it evolved under the adverse conditions of harsh weather, scarce food and hard work, the Canadian Horse remains the sturdiest and most acclimatized horse in Canada today: tough, strong, tolerant of inclement weather conditions and an extremely "easy keeper". Because of these traits, the Canadian is often referred to as "The Little Iron Horse".

Over a hundred years ago, the historian Taillon described the Canadian Horse in these words: *"small, but robust, hocks of steel, thick mane floating in the wind, bright and lively eyes, pricking its sen-*

sitive ears at the least noise, going along day and night with the same courage, wide awake beneath its harness; spirited, good, gentle, affectionate, following his road with the finest instinct to come surely home to his own stable. Such were the horses of our fathers."

ANNE METIKOSH is the author of *Terra Incognita*, a young adult historical novel set in 1670 New France. Her research for that story introduced her to the history of the Canadian Horse. Anne lives in Calgary, Alberta, and although she does not own a Canadian Horse, she does own and ride a beautiful mare named Genie.

↶ THE BEAR TREE (page 72)

Marguerite Sédilot's betrothal, when she was just eleven years and five months old, made her the youngest known bride-to-be in Canadian history. She and Jean Aubuchon had their first child, a boy, Médéric, on August 7, 1660. Four more boys followed before Marguerite had her Marie, in 1671. The couple had 14 children together, though not all of them lived past infancy. Jean Aubuchon died in 1685. Widows often remarried in New France and, in 1687, Marguerite wed her second husband, Pierre Lusseau. The Lusseaus had one child, a son named Pierre, the following year. Marguerite Lusseau died in 1710, at the age of 67.

In Marguerite's day, child brides were not uncommon in France and its colonies. Before 1660 the average age of brides in New France was fifteen. Samuel de Champlain, the "Father of New France", married a twelve-year-old girl, Hélène Boullé, in France in 1610. When Marguerite and Jean married in 1655, there were at least six times as many men as women in New France. It would be nine more years before the first ship carrying *filles du roi* or "king's daughters" arrived, bringing women from France who would choose their own husbands from the colony's many bachelors.

VICTORIA MILES is the author of several books for children, including the bestselling *Sea Otter Pup* (Orca Book Publishers). She lives in Vancouver, British Columbia. In 1998, Victoria was writer-in-residence for the Grafton Historical Society in Grafton, Vermont where she learned that pioneers used bear grease for lamp oil, their children drank watery (but most certainly alcoholic) apple cider and not much blooms in mud season — apart from pussywillows.

Ꭷ— FAREWELL THE MOHAWK VALLEY (page 86)

Canadians frequently see their own history through American eyes. This is especially true in the case of the American Revolution. To start with, Canadians are often unaware that the conflict was almost as much a civil war as a revolution, with colonists who wanted the Thirteen Colonies to remain British fighting other colonists who wanted an independent country. The former were referred to as Tories or Loyalists, the latter as Whigs or Rebels. Obviously, "Tory" and "Whig" did not mean what they mean today.

The American Declaration of Independence was adopted on July 4, 1776, although hostilities had begun in the previous year. The British forces consisted of British and Loyalist soldiers, allied with Indian warriors. Some of the soldiers were as young as twelve years of age. Upon enlisting, a soldier was given a silver coin called a shilling. "Taking the King's shilling" was like signing a contract.

When the fighting began, it looked as though the British would win. The tide turned in 1777. The British had planned a triple invasion, with three armies converging at Albany, New York. General Burgoyne's army came down from the north, expecting to meet an army coming from the east and one coming from the west. If it had worked, the British would have won the war. But the other two armies failed to arrive. General Burgoyne's army, outnumbered

20,000 to 6,000 and exhausted after days of fighting, surrendered at Saratoga on October 17, 1777.

For several years there had been discrimination against Loyalists, and it became worse after the Battle of Saratoga. Roaming gangs who called themselves the Sons of Liberty, or Liberty men, physically attacked Loyalists, stole their property and burned their homes without fear of the law. It was as if motorcycle gangs were allowed to commit any crime they wished, as long as it was against one specific group of people.

The Sons of Liberty brought destruction and terror to the Mohawk Valley, an area of prosperous farms and small communities located along the Mohawk River in what is now upper New York State. After General Burgoyne's defeat, many Whigs there turned upon their Tory neighbours. Communities and families were torn apart. Some Loyalists were driven away; others fled. Most escaped north to Canada.

British forts along the border took in Loyalist refugees. One of these forts was on Carleton Island, situated between the south shore of the St. Lawrence River and Wolfe Island, only a few miles from the present city of Kingston, Ontario. Many Loyalist families who made their way through dense forests to reach a British fort would have perished without the help of the Mohawks, one of the Six Nations of the Iroquois Confederacy.

Among the most important Loyalists from the Mohawk Valley were Sir John Johnson and the Reverend John Stuart. Sir John was a wealthy young landowner who led a party of refugees to safety in Montréal, then raised two battalions of soldiers to fight on the British side. The Reverend Stuart was an Anglican minister whose church at Fort Hunter had been attended by both Indians and white settlers. After losing his liberty because of the help he gave to Loyalists, he was sent to Canada as part of an exchange of prisoners of war. He is remembered as the Father of the Church in Upper Canada (Ontario) and as the founder of that province's first school, which still exists as Kingston Collegiate and Vocational Institute.

JEAN RAE BAXTER wanted to be a writer ever since her teens, when the *Hamilton Spectator* paid her one dollar per column inch for covering high school events. After graduating from university, she had three successive careers: working in radio, teaching English, and developing educational programs for an Anglican cathedral. The writing of articles, plays and poems was something she did on the side. Finally, three years ago, she made the decision to focus on writing full time. Her story "The Quilt" was awarded first prize in the *Canadian Writer's Journal* 2000 Short Fiction Competition. She is now working on a collection of short stories and has two novels nearing completion. Jean lives in Hamilton, Ontario.

∿ RULE OF SILENCE (page 99)

The Provincial Penitentiary of Upper Canada (renamed Kingston Penitentiary after Confederation), built in 1835 and still in use to-day, enforced a rule of silence for almost a hundred years. Although the warden in this story is fictitious, Antoine was real and he was tiny — under four feet tall. He was not by any means the only child to be sent to this penitentiary, but he *was* the youngest, the first and only eight-year-old to be imprisoned there. Records in the Punishment Book show that he was lashed shortly after he arrived and then 47 more times over the next nine months. According to David St. Onge, Curator of the Correctional Service of Canada Museum who first told me of the child-prisoners, the youngest female inmate of Kingston Penitentiary was nine-year-old Sarah Jane Pierce. She spent seven years there for stealing a quilt, a water pitcher, a bonnet and some biscuits.

In the 1800s it was believed that long-term imprisonment combined with hard work, prayers, silence, strict rules and harsh and frequent punishments would reform prisoners; that after their sentences had been served they would return to society as honest citizens. The Punishment Book of Kingston Penitentiary records hundreds of beatings with the cat-o'-nine-tails (a thick strap with eight smaller strands attached to it) or the leather (rawhide) lash, days spent without any food except bread and water and hours locked in the "dark box" which looked like an upright coffin. The Rule of Silence was enforced strictly. Prisoners, young and older, were punished for talking, whistling, laughing and for many other reasons (including winking), most of which would not be considered serious offences today, either in penitentiaries or in schools!

Whipping continued to be a legal punishment in our country well into the middle of the twentieth century; the leather strap was used in Canadian schools until the 1970s. And, although long sentences in jail have been shown not to work, not to "cure" offenders (instead penitentiaries are often called "training grounds" for young criminals) modern penitentiaries remain full.

ANN WALSH is the author of five historical novels: *Your Time, My Time; Moses Me and Murder; The Ghost of Soda Creek; The Doctor's Apprentice;* and *Shabash!* She has also written a book of poetry and is the editor of *Winds Through Time (An Anthology of Canadian Historical Young Adult Fiction)* published in 1998. Her stories for younger readers include one about Alzheimer's disease which has appeared in several anthologies and textbooks, and her short fiction for adults has been published in magazines and newspapers around the world. Ann lives in Williams Lake, B.C.

ࢽ THE FIRST SPIKE (page 114)

The Canadian Pacific Railway, the longest railway in the world at the time, was completed in 1885. It linked western Canada with eastern Canada, and brought British Columbia into Confederation. The symbolism of the Last Spike was made much of by politicians then and by writers and poets ever since.

The promise of a railway between British Columbia and Ontario was made in 1871 when British Columbia agreed to join Canada. The promise was backed by Prime Minister John A. Macdonald, who thought that such a link would keep the western territories safe from the encroaching United States. The railway became the center of the "Pacific Scandal" in 1873 when Macdonald was accused of corruption and resigned.

Work began on the Canadian Pacific Railway in 1875 at Fort William, Ontario. It joined with other, shorter railways that spread throughout Eastern Canada. The CPR was built towards the west from Ontario and towards the east from British Columbia. Thousands of workers were brought over from China. These workers were underpaid, underfed, and ill-housed. Many died. The abuse of these workers was overlooked in the glory of completing the longest railway in the world in less than fifteen years.

At Craigellachie, in the Rockies, the line moving east from Ontario met the line moving west. The last spike was driven on the 7th of November, 1885 and, with much fanfare, the connection was made that bound the west to the east.

While much has been written about the CPR, little has been written about the humble beginnings of the railways in British North America. The first Canadian railway was completed in Lower Canada in 1836, and connected La Prairie on the St. Lawrence River to St. Johns on the Richelieu River. It was built initially as a 14-mile segment bypassing some rapids on the river, and eventually connected the two towns. The first Canadian locomotive, the Dorchester, made its maiden voyage, at a speed of 23 kilometers per hour, along the La Prairie to St. Johns route on July 31, 1836.

LAURA MORGAN is an elementary school teacher who lives in Prince Rupert, British Columbia, with her husband and two children. This is her first published story.

〜 A GOURMET DINES AT THE END OF TRACK (page 128)

In 1871 British Columbia joined Confederation on the promise of a rail link to the rest of Canada. On November 7, 1885 the last spike on the Canadian Pacific Railway Company's transcontinental line was driven at Craigellachie, B.C.

The building of a railway across the continent was a tremendous undertaking for the small, new country of Canada. John A. Macdonald and other political leaders of the day believed that a railway linking the established east, the raw new west and the far-off colony of British Columbia was necessary to ensure that the western lands did not become part of the United States of America.

William Cornelius Van Horne, who was appointed General Manager of the Canadian Pacific Railway Company in 1881, shared their vision. While other men were responsible for obtaining the finances to pay for the railway and managing the political scene, Van Horne was in charge of getting the rails laid and the trains moving.

The Canadian Pacific Railway was to be built in sections with separate contractors in charge. Compared to the extremely difficult terrain of the Canadian Shield, the Rocky Mountains and most of British Columbia, the laying of the line across the prairies was relatively easy. In fifteen months, the work gangs, driven by the vigilant and autocratic General Manager, laid 600 miles of track between

Winnipeg and Calgary. "The end of track" or "end of steel" were terms used to describe the location of the camps out of which the men worked. On the prairies the camp shifted frequently as the rails moved westward.

The work gangs, made up of immigrants from many countries, were only one part of a highly efficient enterprise all organized and overseen by the General Manager. Van Horne took an interest in every aspect of the operation and frequently made unannounced tours of inspection to all parts of the work. Viewed by many as a tyrant, Van Horne was at the same time a brilliant manager, a financier, an intellectual, an amateur artist of great ability and a gourmet. Born in Illinois, Van Horne became President of the Canadian Pacific Railway in 1888 and made his home in Montréal for the rest of his life.

CONSTANCE HORNE was born and educated in Winnipeg. She taught Canadian history in high schools in Manitoba and British Columbia. She feels privileged to have travelled several times over the prairies and through the mountains on the CPR between Winnipeg and Vancouver. Eating in the dining car was a highlight of each trip.

Constance Horne now lives in Victoria, B.C. She is the author of *Nykola and Granny, The Jo Boy Deserts, Trapped by Coal, Emily Carr's Woo, The Accidental Orphan, Lost in the Blizzard* and *The Tenth Pupil.*

ᏌᎳ PROMISES AND POSSIBILITIES (page 141)

From the mid-1800s until the beginning of the First World War in 1914, thousands of homesteaders to Canada made their way west. Most were lured by the promise of cheap, plentiful prairie land. In the early 1900s, major cities in the British Isles were flooded by colourful pamphlets extolling the beauty and wealth to be found in the Canadian prairies. England was experiencing an economic depression, forcing many out of work, and the promise of land and standing was hard to resist. While the plentiful cheap land promised was definitely to be found, other virtues of the prairies cited, such as peach and apple orchards, high yields of grain, bubbling streams, were not. As the pamphlets were distributed in cities, many of the homesteaders had never farmed in their lives. They arrived to find a mosquito-infested, vast grassland prairie, the ground so hard a plow could barely break the sod. Wives were shocked to discover they had to live in sod houses built of dirt and grass and that the only fuel to be had was animal dung. Fingers that had known needlework were suddenly pulling up sod, fetching water from far-off sloughs, making soap and candles and all household necessities and, once that was done, planting gardens and driving horses harnessed to plows. Some would-be settlers found the freezing prairie winter, the mind-numbing isolation and constant uncertainty of crop success too difficult to be borne and admitted defeat and returned to their homeland. Most saw the possibilities and promises in their newly adopted land and stayed to become Canada's pioneers. An excellent website for this material can be found at www.lloydminster.net/Chapter1.htm.

BARBARA HAWORTH-ATTARD is the author of eight middle-grade and young adult novels, four of which are historical: *Dark of the Moon, Home Child, Love-Lies-Bleeding,* all from Roussan Publishers, and *Flying Geese,* from HarperCollins Canada. Her other work includes one contemporary young adult novel, *Buried Treasure,* and two middle-grade fantasies, *TruthSinger* and its sequel, *Wynd-Magic,* all from Roussan Publishers. Barbara also writes short stories. She lives in London, Ontario.

୨– SONGS FOR THE DEAD (page 151)

Coal mining in the depths of the mountains was a dangerous occupation. Working in almost complete darkness, miners were often hurt by falling rock, loose coal, collapsing tunnels and other natural hazards. In addition, the presence of lethal methane gas and volatile coal dust posed a constant threat of explosion.

Miners carried their own light into the mines. In the Crowsnest Pass region of southern Alberta, in the early 1900s, most miners used either the open-flame carbide lamps or the safety lamps. The open-flame lamp cast a stronger light but presented a greater danger of explosion. These lamps were especially dangerous when the level of methane in the mine was high. For that reason, some miners preferred the safety lamps, which, although dimmer, kept the flame safely confined and cooled it below the ignition temperature of methane. In addition, the appearance of a pale blue cap of burning gas around the lamp's yellow flame indicated the presence of methane, making it possible to detect lethal pockets of gas before they overcame a man. It took only minutes for methane gas to render a man unconscious and often, within minutes, dead. Birds, with their small lung capacity, were particularly susceptible to methane gas and were sometimes used as sacrificial indicators in Canadian mines.

"Songs for the Dead" is loosely based on a series of explosions in the mines of the Crowsnest Pass region in the early 1900s. In this area, the use of safety lamps was controversial, and the coal companies were reluctant to implement these precautions. However, in 1907, the Provincial Mines Branch made safety lamps mandatory throughout Alberta.

"Songs for the Dead" is the story of Jonathon, who found the courage to speak out, and his father, who chose, for the first time, to listen to his son's advice. Although they are fictional, their characters are based on the real, documented lives of miners and their families in the Crowsnest Pass area who courageously confronted the darkness of the coal mines day after day.

CATHY BEVERIDGE is the author of numerous young adult short stories, published in various anthologies. She is also the author/editor of two literary anthologies entitled *Wellness,* published in 1994, and *Cultures in Transition,* published in 1995. Her first young adult novel, entitled *Offside,* will be published in 2001. As a young girl, Cathy spent many summers in the Crowsnest Pass area where her great-grandparents were once coal miners. She currently lives in Calgary, Alberta with her husband and three daughters.

∽— THE BALLOT (page 163)

Elizabeth McLennan, her father Alistair and their neighbour Edna Holmes are all fictitious characters. But the beliefs expressed by Elizabeth's father in "The Ballot" were widely held at one time in Canada. And the election at which Elizabeth cast her first ballot actually occurred across Ontario on October 20, 1919. Voters, especially women, showed up in full force to decide on electoral candidates and on the fate of the Ontario Temperance Act, a measure put into place by Sir William Hearst's Conservative Government to rid society of alcohol consumption. When the ballots were tallied, the majority overwhelmingly favoured prohibition. Sir William, however, was defeated. For the women of Ontario, it was the first provincial election in which they were permitted a vote.

Before the early 1900s, the women of the Dominion of Canada did not vote in either provincial or federal elections. It was not by choice. According to the Election Act, "no woman, idiot, lunatic, or criminal" had the right to a ballot. The idea of women achieving the vote was considered scandalous. It was believed that extending the franchise would destroy men's chivalry toward women and could only result in the destruction of marriage and family life. Women at the turn of the twentieth century had few rights of any kind and were not officially considered "persons" under the law until 1929. Clearly the early suffragists had their work cut out.

The suffrage movement in Canada was initiated in Ontario. Among the first to campaign for political equality was Dr. Emily Howard Stowe, Canada's first woman doctor. Barred from entering medical schools because of her sex, Dr. Stowe completed her training in New York. Upon her return to Canada, she practised medicine and took up the cause of women's rights. As early as 1867, Dr. Stowe organized the first suffrage group under the camouflage of a literary club. Members of this group met in Toronto and discussed the need for the ballot, seeing this as the lever to other reforms.

So what happened?

The movement grew. Suffragists took on the task of educating the public — both men and women — in the need for reform. Letter-writing campaigns and determined petitioning of legislatures began. Between 1916, when Manitoba women first won the right to vote in a provincial election, and 1940, when their Quebec counterparts achieved the franchise, women in every province achieved the right to vote in provincial elections. By 1918, all Canadian women over the age of twenty-one were allowed to vote in federal elections. One of the most compelling arguments for extending the franchise was the service and competence of Canadian women during the First World War.

CATHERINE GOODWIN is the co-author of *Growing Up, Reaching Out* (Modulo Editeur, 1999). She also writes and edits material for English Second Language textbooks and has written articles for newspapers and magazines. Originally from Montréal, Catherine now lives with her family in London, Ontario. "The Ballot" is her first published historical short story.

⌒ TO BEGIN AGAIN (page 175)

Between 1870 and 1930, 100,000 destitute, orphaned or illegitimate British children were sent to Canada to begin new lives. The people who arranged this believed that the children would have a better chance at life in a new country where there was fresh air, work, good food and plenty of open space. A few of the younger children were adopted by Canadian families. Most, however, were trained in England so they could work in Canada. The boys trained as carpenters, harness-makers and blacksmiths. In Canada, most of them worked on farms. The girls trained to become domestic servants and mother's helpers.

The stories of the lives of these "Home Children" is told in several books for adult and younger readers, and by family members who remember. For some children, their chance at a new life was a wonderful opportunity. For others, their lives became nightmares because they were beaten, discriminated against or abused. The incident where Gwen throws hot dishwater at a man intent on hurting her, is a true story.

The picture frame containing flowers woven from human hair was common in Victorian England and Canada. "Mourning wreaths", like the one described, or "mourning brooches" which were a tiny version of the same thing, were memorials to a deceased loved one, woven from the dead person's hair.

Pauline Johnson-Tekahionwake must have been inspiring to her audiences. In a time when white women couldn't even vote, she was making her own living, travelling and literally "paddling her own canoe". Pauline was born in 1861 at Chiefswood on the Six Nations Reserve in Ontario. Her mother was English and her father was a

Mohawk chief. Pauline began writing as a child. In her twenties, her poetry was published in newspapers and magazines. In 1892 Pauline began performing her poetry on stage. She was billed as "Canada's Foremost Comedienne and Poetess" and "The Mohawk Poet Reciter". Between 1892 and 1910, Pauline performed from Newfoundland to British Columbia, in the USA and in London, England. Her unique poetry focussed partly on the relationship between Native and non-Native peoples. Her stage appearances were unique, too. For the first half of her show she wore a typical, fashionable dress. For the second half she wore a fringed buckskin dress trimmed with fur and a wampum belt, and a bear claw necklace. Her most famous poem is "The Song My Paddle Sings".

"To Begin Again" is one story from a novel-in-process called "Gwen".

CAROLYN POGUE is the author of four books, including *A Creation Story*, a picture book for children. Her work also includes plays, articles, poetry, nonfiction and short fiction for both children and adults. She has edited elementary school textbooks and teachers' guides for use in Ontario, Alberta and the Northwest Territories. Carolyn currently works with children in grades 3 to 6 as a volunteer in the Partners in Literacy Program.

Carolyn is the granddaughter of a Home Child who arrived in Canada, aged twelve, in 1898. Carolyn and her daughter, Andrea, recently travelled to the Barnardo Home in England to celebrate their ancestor's courage. Carolyn lives in Calgary, Alberta.

∽ MAGIC, PURE MAGIC (page 187)

Raymond Munro was born in Montreal, Quebec, in 1921. He and his brother Roy both became fighter pilots in the Royal Canadian Air Force during WW II. After leaving the armed forces, Raymond worked for the *Toronto Star* as an award-winning photographer. When his wife died, he brought his two children and his mother and father west to Vancouver. He became a reporter/photographer with the *Vancouver Sun,* joining a team of journalists that included Pierre Berton and Jack Webster. In his autobiography, Webster recalls a trip he and Raymond took to a train crash in the Fraser Canyon. Raymond, who was piloting them in a small plane, made a spectacular run, flying down inside the canyon walls, shooting footage of the train wreck while holding the joy-stick between his knees. Pierre Berton remembers Munro as a real character who had his car rigged up with red lights and sirens and ambulance equipment. In 1947, Raymond and his partner, Art Jones, had the first radio-telephone car in Vancouver. The equipment weighed fifty pounds and could be operated while the car was stationary or moving. Raymond Munro was instrumental in apprehending a serial rapist and exposing corruption in the Vancouver Police Department. He left Vancouver shortly after The Tupper Inquiry, and went on to many and varied adventures, including touring the country as a hypnotist. Raymond's more predictable adventures revolved around aerial photography, parachute jumping, balloon flying and bush piloting. Flying dominated his life. He received the Order of Canada in 1973 for promoting Canada's Aviation Hall of Fame and was the curator of the Edmonton Flight Museum for several years before he died of cancer in 1994.

Ray's brother Roy died in a low-level flight, undertaking a special night time mission across the North Sea during the Second World War. His aircraft, a Beaufighter, suffered a direct hit from an anti-aircraft gun. Raymond received word of his brother's death on Christmas Eve, 1944.